A sound knifed through his thoughts, halting him suddenly. Not from inside the Boyd suite, but not far away. Muffled by a thick door. A woman's scream.

Novak sprinted down the corridor, halting in front of 516. One hand fingered the master key in his pocket as he pressed an ear against the door panel. From inside, a man's voice snarling indistinguishable words, a woman whimpering. Then the hard crack of flesh on flesh.

Novak thumbed the door button and his hands folded into fists.

The door opened. A man peered out. "Yeah?" he bristled. "Beat it."

He made an effort to slam the door but Novak's foot blocked it. Leaning forward, Novak heaved his shoulder and the door burst inward. The man staggered back cursing.

"I'm Novak. Hotel Security. Where's the woman?"

To see her, all he had to do was glance sideways and down. Her back was braced against the edge of a chair, her legs folded under her thighs. She wore a filmy white dressing gown, one sleeve ripped. Her cheeks showed ugly patches of red, the rest of her face was bloodless. She must have been in the shower when the guy came in because the dressing gown was all she wore. The legs were nicely muscled and they melted into slim thighs. Her stomach was taut and she had never been a nursing mother.

The man dropped his head and lunged...

House
DICK

by **E. Howard Hunt**

A HARD CASE CRIME NOVEL

A HARD CASE CRIME BOOK
(HCC-054)
April 2009

Published by

Dorchester Publishing Co., Inc.
200 Madison Avenue
New York, NY 10016

in collaboration with Winterfall LLC

This book is a work of fiction. Names, characters, places, and incidents either are the products of the author's imagination or are used fictitiously, and any resemblance to actual events or persons, living or dead, is entirely coincidental.

ISBN 0-8439-6116-3
ISBN-13 978-0-8439-6116-4

Cover design by Cooley Design Lab

Typeset by Swordsmith Productions

The name "Hard Case Crime" and the Hard Case Crime logo are trademarks of Winterfall LLC. Hard Case Crime books are selected and edited by Charles Ardai.

Printed in the United States of America

Visit us on the web at www.HardCaseCrime.com

HOUSE DICK

1

Pete Novak eased his six-foot, hundred-and-eighty-four-pound frame through the revolving entrance door of the Hotel Tilden and saw a girl in a platinum mink coat walking toward the reception desk. Beside her a bellhop struggled with three gray leather bags. The girl was an ash blonde and Novak could catch the scent of light perfume following in her wake. From her gray-gloved hand a gray leather leash slanted down to the collar of a toy Skye terrier. The girl walked with her head thrown back, her heels making subdued clicking sounds on the marble floor of the lobby. What little of her legs could be seen looked promising. The terrier stopped short, braced his paws and yipped protestingly. The girl looked down at him and Novak saw that her eyes were as gray as the furs she wore. As the leash around her wrist. As the luggage Jimmy Grant was wrestling with. Novak sniffed her perfume once more, patted a small package in his side pocket, grinned and decided to stick around.

Novak took out a cigarette, lighted it and watched her register. The clerk flattened his palms on the marble counter, stood on tiptoes and peered over at the terrier. He said something to the girl and Novak saw her frown. He decided to move closer.

The girl was saying, "...but I can't possibly stay

without Toby. Can't you make an exception just this once?"

"No, ma'am," the clerk said firmly. "No animals at the Tilden. Not even a canary."

Novak grinned and said, "Not even a bedbug, miss."

Her head moved quickly to one side, and cool gray eyes appraised him. Her red lips were full and even, her nose straight and her cheekbones high. The gray eyes were almond-shaped, as though at some time, generations back, Indian blood had entered the family strain. Her tawny skin supported the thought.

He glanced down at the registration card and saw that she had written: *Paula Norton, Muncie, Ind.* The Mr. and Mrs. boxes had been x-ed out. That made her a Miss. For the record.

Slowly and with an edge her voice articulated, "I guess there's one in every hotel."

"Bedbug?"

Ash blonde hair swirled as she turned away. To the clerk she snapped, "We were talking about my dog."

The clerk started to sputter but Novak cut in. "Let's put him up at Dr. Robinson's, Miss Norton. The doc's got a fine place not two blocks away—just a short walk—in case you miss Toby and want to run over and visit him."

Her head turned again. She smiled and said dryly, "Now it comes to me. You're a shill for a dog hospital."

The clerk bent toward her stiffly. "Our Mr. Novak, Miss Norton. House Security Service."

Novak took off his hat and fingered the brim. "Also Assistant Personnel Manager, Miss Norton."

Her lips twisted. "Another way of saying house dick."

"Yeah," Novak said indifferently. "Personnel hires them and I fire them. That way we keep all the work in the same office. Efficient."

"I'm sure I wouldn't know," she said coolly, "never having worked in a hotel." Bending over, she scooped up the Skye and deposited it in Novak's arms. "Here," she said, "*you* take care of him, Mr. Novak—since you're such a close friend of Dr. Robinson's." Then she turned, jerked her head at the bellhop and glided across the lobby toward the elevator. Jimmy Grant stared at Novak, snickered, and picked up her bags. The desk clerk hurried around the far side of the counter and gave the room key to the bellboy. Elevator doors opened, Miss Norton entered and Jimmy followed. Novak frowned. The clerk came back and the nails of his right hand made a scaly sound against the palm. In a nervous voice he said, "You've been warned about taking liberties with the guests."

Novak sighed. "True, Percy. Only too true. But with guests of Miss Norton's special qualifications I'm a habitual offender; try as I may to resist, it's hopeless." Gathering the terrier into a small furry bundle, he pressed it on the clerk. "Be a good fellow and call Doc Robinson, huh? Let's give our guests a little service."

Then he turned, brushed Skye hair from his arms, smoothed his tie and walked around the end of the reception counter toward a door marked *Personnel*.

He tossed his hat at a stand in the corner, pulled off his coat and opened the Venetian blinds. Gray light from K Street filtered into his office. Novak lighted the lamp on his desk, sucked a lungful of smoke from his cigarette, butted it. Then he pulled a small envelope from his coat pocket, laid it on his desk and sat down. One hand pressed the intercom button and he spoke to the Tilden's chief engineer.

"Mike, Pete Novak. You got a mech working for you named MacDonald—plumbing and air conditioning. Well, tell him to scoot up and see me. Yeah, he's off at eight, but this can't wait. If he asks what's up tell him it's about his family. Okay."

Snapping off the intercom Novak unsnapped the butt strap of his shoulder holster and drew out a snubnose .38. He laid it on his desk near the brown envelope. Squinting in the semi-dark of his office he turned slowly in his chair until he faced the window. Early spring in Washington with fog and light drizzles. The sound of tires on wet paving, the muffled honking of horns through gray, heavy air. The Girl in Gray, Novak thought. Then he heard a noise and turned.

The man who came through the door was as big as Novak, and he wore blue coveralls with *Hotel Tilden* stitched across the chest. His hair was light blonde and curly. He wore round, steel-rimmed glasses and there were squint lines across his forehead and at the corners of his eyes. He said, "I'm MacDonald. You want to see me?"

Novak indicated a chair. When MacDonald settled uneasily into it, Novak said, "Ask me why you're here, Murky."

MacDonald's eyes narrowed. "You tell me, copper.

What's the rap?" His eyes flickered toward the envelope, the blue steel revolver.

Novak leaned forward, laid his arms on the desk and said softly, "This hotel chain's run by a bunch of humanitarians, Murky. Either that or there's a labor shortage I haven't heard about. Your application came in, I checked the files and found you'd done a dipsey. For me that disqualified you, but the management hired you anyway, on the basis that you wouldn't have contact with the public."

MacDonald's face was working. "It was a rib-up," he husked. "They give me a two-specker on a rib-up."

"Can the excuses," Novak said. "The boarding schools are bulging with guys who got a bum rap—to hear them tell it. But passing over your last sorrowful tale brings me to a theft that took place here at the Tilden only two weeks ago. A lady from Cleveland, Murky. A blonde divorcée silly enough to stuff some jewels in a desk drawer and waltz down to dinner. Next day when she looked for the dazzlers, guess what? Some were missing." His left hand lifted the brown envelope and spilled the contents on the desk. Light flashed from a jeweled bracelet, two rings and a sparkling brooch. "Finders keepers?" he said in a smooth, needling voice.

MacDonald's face was the color of bleached bone. His right hand clawed at the throat of his coverall. He half-rose from the chair.

Novak shook his head disgustedly. "Not even half-smart, Murky. The gal put in a beef about her air conditioning and the record shows you were the mech who went up to fix it—while she was having her mountain trout and vin rosé." He sighed, shifted in his chair and his ring hand moved an inch closer to the butt of his .38. "Tell me I needed a search warrant to shake down your room, Murky. Tell me you don't have a glimmer how the loot got taped behind your bureau." His throat made an unpleasant sound. "On your way, punk. No pink slip for you. Just out. And park the monkey suit in the locker room. It's hotel property."

MacDonald was standing, hands clenching and unclenching. He looked like a sick man. "Give me a break," he whispered.

Novak said, "You got it, Murky. And give me a prayer of thanks tonight. If I turned you in it'd be a tenner this time. And you got kids. As it stands, the dame'll get the jewels back and be forever grateful. If you've got an ounce of sense you'll feel the same. *Raus!*"

MacDonald turned and groped like a sleepwalker toward the door. It opened, sounds from the lobby drifted through, the moving body blocked the light and then the door closed.

Novak's face twisted into a wry grimace. After a while he got up, patted the .38 back into the shoulder holster and went over to a file safe. He turned the dial combination until a drawer opened and then he went back, returned the jewelry to the envelope, licked the flap, sealed it, and dropped it inside the drawer. Then he opened another drawer, one with employee record cards, and made a notation on one. The file banged shut.

Outside it was darker now. Novak pulled out a key

chain and unlocked a low drawer in his metal desk. He
fumbled for a moment and pulled out a pint bottle of
Irish whisky. Uncapping it, he swallowed an ounce,
rolled it around his tongue and let it drain slowly down
his throat. He swallowed another ounce, sighed and
replaced the bottle. Then he locked the drawer. Mock-
ingly he announced: "Employees will not drink alco-
holic beverages while on duty," wiped his mouth on
the sleeve of his shirt and opened the door of a small
bathroom. Clicking on the electric razor he buzzed his
face lightly. It was a face that looked as if it had seen its
share of trouble. Broad forehead, nose laced with fine
scars of plastic repair, a lateral scar just under his right
eye that could have been made by a slammed hockey
puck or brass knuckles; heavy, dark-brown eyebrows
over deep-set brown eyes; brown hair streaked with
silver; and white teeth that were even only because
they had been broken, ground down and capped. The
hand that guided the razor showed flat, powerful fingers with knuckles enlarged by violent impact, broad
nails trimmed short and square.

His hand tested the side of his face for stubble, then
clicked the razor off. When he had washed he began to
hum a disconnected tune, went into his office and
pulled on his coat. Novak liked the feel of the finished
worsted; it had been a two-hundred-dollar suit marked
down on an off-season sale three years before. The few
suits he had were of good quality and tailoring. His
brown, pebble-grain brogues had cost close to forty
dollars six years ago. He had a matching pair in black
for hotel reception work, patent leathers for black-tie

hotel parties and a pair of suede chukka boots for off-duty wear. Novak was a man who traveled light but what little he carried was as good as he could buy.

Nearly seven o'clock. He closed the blinds on the dark street, turned and peered across the dim office at his secretary's empty desk. Mary had checked out at five, but his job knew no hours. At five o'clock he had been bluffing Murky's landlady into letting him search the mechanic's room for a mythical set of hotel keys. Maybe tonight some guy would pull a Dutchman and a frantic clerk would screech him down to the hotel before the cops arrived. Or a chippy would be entertaining gentleman callers at so much a head. Not at the Tilden, sister. Peddle it somewhere else. Hell, in a three-hundred-and-forty-room hotel anything could happen.

As he turned off the desk lamp he felt a chill creep through the office. A lonely place. At this hour very lonely. The Lost and Found Department, only you had to handle more than compacts and wallets and forgotten razors. Drunks too drunk to remember who they were or who rolled them, badger game couples, barroom hustlers, check artists, high-class panhandlers, con men, maids with larcenous fingers, pimping bell-hops…Novak moistened his lips, grabbed his hat and jammed his hands into his pockets. A sweet job—like garbage collecting.

As he opened the door to the lobby he muttered to himself, "Well, you promised Mother you'd have a white-collar job," and closed the door quietly.

Novak's heels clicked across lobby marble as he

walked toward the hotel exit. Beside him Jimmy Grant materialized. "Gee, Pete, what a dish that Miss Norton, huh?"

"Sure is. Now get the gleam out of your eyes, sonny."

"New luggage, Pete. Had that store smell. And heavy. Boy, them bags musta had a dozen gold ingots apiece."

"Legit?"

The hop shrugged. "Could be. No ring and not a society broad."

"Why not?"

"She slipped me two bucks. Them's that really got it don't paper the streets with the stuff. Not this year."

Novak tapped his cheek lightly. "You might make an investigator at that."

Jimmy grinned. "Boy, did you look funny holding that pup she shoved at you. I didn't hear no fast comeback, neither."

"There's a time for throwaway dialogue and a time to hold silence. That's life, kiddo." He moved on and out to the sidewalk. He turned down K Street, bought a *Star* from the kid on the corner and flagged a passing cab.

Between courses at the *ristorante italiano* out on New York Avenue he thumbed through the evening paper. Mama brought over a chianti bottle wrapped in straw and said, "I like you to try, Pete. Just offa the boat."

"I don't go much for wine, Mama. Been kicked in the belly too much."

"*Si*, but this different." Uncorking it she filled a small glass, poured another for herself. It had the thin

clear taste of good red house wine. Novak said so.
Mama smiled. "Beats anything French, Pete. Here,
you keep the bottle."

"Some other night, Mama."

"Okay." She corked it. "This your bottle, remember."

"I'll remember."

"And bring a girl." Her eyebrows furrowed. "Alla
time you come alone. Why you never bring girl? Food
not good enough?"

Novak managed a laugh. "Hell, it's the best food
in town. A girl? I had a girl once. Maybe once was
enough."

Mama frowned. Her lips opened to say something
but a waiter hurried up with a steaming plate of *scaloppine*. Novak tucked a napkin under his chin and started
in. When he looked up again Mama was back at the
cash register watching the bartender thoughtfully.

No movies he wanted to see, no fights in town. Not
even an automobile show at the Armory. Too early in
the year for open-air concerts at Watergate. Nothing
to do but go back to his apartment and read, or clean
his .38. As he walked along the sidewalk he decided he
ought to return to the hotel and write a file memorandum on Murky MacDonald for circulation to the hotel
protective association. Mary could cut a stencil and
have it mailed by mid-morning. Then he could sleep
late and to hell with the Tilden.

A legless bum was propped against a lamppost,
formless as a battered trash can. Novak dropped a
quarter in the reaching hand and passed on, setting his
lips at the husky thanks. A hustler strolled furtively in

the shadows, shiny patent-leather purse, a ruby glow tipping her cigarette. He shrugged her aside and walked on. From a bar came raucous laughter, the drone of a TV program turned up too loud, the stench of stale beer hugging the spring night.

At the corner he piled into a cab and rode back to the Tilden. Percy was still at the desk. When he saw Novak he waved his pen like a conductor's baton and shrilled, "Thank goodness you've come, Mr. Novak. The most terrible thing has happened!"

Novak pushed back his hat. "Beetles in the flower shop, Percy?"

The clerk flushed and made a distracted gesture with one hand. "Please, Mr. Novak, this is no time for joking."

"For me it is," Novak said sourly. "I went off duty hours ago." He turned and scanned the lobby. "See? I'm not even here."

"Of course you're here. And the guest in 515 needs your services. Oh, very badly. All of her jewels are missing."

2

Suite 515 drew thirty-five dollars a day plus District tax and it had been redecorated at a time when Mayan motifs were all the rage among the decorator set. The furniture was angular wood-and-metal, and around the rust-colored carpet crawled a feathered serpent calculated to resemble a frieze of gray volcanic stone. What the place lacked in fireside comfort it made up in tony design.

Mrs. Chalmers Boyd was a tinted brunette in the mid-forties with bon-bon jowls and arms like rolls of biscuit dough. Her fleshy feet were jammed into pointed slippers two sizes too small and her face was heavily powdered to improve an uncertain complexion. The registration card put her and her husband from Winnetka, Illinois, with a double-A rating marked by the credit office. For a lady who was missing a small fortune in jewels, Mrs. Chalmers Boyd had herself under perfect control. No smelling salts, no house physician administering sedatives. Nothing. She looked as placid as a brewer's wife.

Novak said, "Suppose you tell me what happened, Mrs. Boyd."

The button nose wrinkled and she said, "They're all insured. Everything. I guess it doesn't matter, does it?"

"The insurance company might be glad of any assistance you could render."

"Oh, yes, I suppose so. Well, I reported the theft to the desk as soon as I discovered it. I'd been shopping, you know—Garfinckels, Rizak's, the usual places. Then when I came back here to dress for dinner I had a sort of a funny feeling about them. Normally I wouldn't have opened the box until I was dressed and ready to select something to wear, but this time I went straight for the jewel box."

"It was kept where, Mrs. Boyd?"

"Why, in one of my suitcases. There, on the luggage rack." A fat arm gestured indifferently.

"Locked?"

The pudgy face moved slowly, negatively. Little eyes glinted mischievously. "I'm afraid not. No...I always tell Chalmers, what's the use of having jewels if you have to keep them locked up all the time? So they're insured. Heavily insured. Why, the annual premiums are a disgrace."

"I can well imagine." Novak got up and walked over to the luggage rack where a heavy rawhide suitcase lay open. One side held frilly nightclothes, the other, twenty or thirty pairs of stockings. As he rumpled through the nylon, Mrs. Boyd said, "Would you care for a drink, Mr. Novak?"

"Thanks, no. You go ahead, though. I bet you could use a bracer about now, Mrs. Boyd."

"Julia," she purred. "Yes, I think I could. All the makings are in the fridge, Mr. Novak. Would you mind terribly?"

"Promise not to tell the bartenders' union," he said and walked into the kitchenette. From the refrigerator he extracted ice cubes, a split of ginger ale and a badly abused bottle of rye. Her voice called, "Not too much ginger."

Novak frowned, built a two-ounce highball and carried it back. Fingers like pale cigars curled around the glass. Her tongue dipped tentatively, Julia Boyd nodded in satisfaction and she suggested that Novak sit down.

He said, "Lost jewelry isn't really my line, Mrs. Boyd, so I won't shake down the place. Naturally the Tilden wants you to have your jewelry back, and if one of our employees is involved we'll do all we can to have it returned. The hotel is insured, of course. By the way, what coverage have you got?"

"Around ninety thousand dollars. The Midland Company in Chicago. Chalmers—that's my husband—is on the board of directors so I don't think there'll be any difficulty about the claim."

Novak nodded. "As a matter of form you'll have to report the loss to the District Police."

"Oh, will that be necessary?" she pouted.

"I'm afraid so. Otherwise the Midland Company might not be obligated to cover your loss. It all depends on the terms of the policy."

She sipped from her glass, rubbed a pudgy finger along the chair arm and said, "It's all so unpleasant, isn't it?"

Novak got up. "Robbery usually is. But the police

here are fairly civilized. They shave and brush their teeth and most of them don't swear in mixed company. When you call, mention the Theft Squad. They'll send someone around."

One finger trailed around the rim of her glass. "Couldn't you do that for me, Mr. Novak?"

"I could, but the police would prefer to hear from you personally."

"Oh. And the insurance company?"

"Your husband will know how to report the loss."

Her eyebrows lifted slightly. "Chalmers? Oh, yes, he'll know. But I was hoping I wouldn't have to involve him."

Novak blinked at her. "My contacts with the moneyed classes have been limited, but I sort of figure Mr. Boyd would be interested in anything affecting his billfold to the extent of ninety grand—taxes being what they are these days."

Her face had gone as blank as white porcelain. "Yes," she said vaguely, sucked at her rye and worried her diamond engagement ring with her thumb. "Thank you, Mr. Novak."

The door buzzed.

Novak looked back at Julia Boyd. She gestured to open the door. Novak clicked the latch free and pulled back on the handle.

The man who stood there wore a suit of ministerial serge, a high glossy collar and a preoccupied expression on his ruddy face. He blinked and craned past Novak's shoulder.

"Mr. Boyd?" Novak asked.

"By no means. My name is Bikel. Dr. Edward Bikel. Where is Mrs. Boyd?" he demanded pompously.

"On the parlor rocker, Doctor. I was just leaving."

Dr. Bikel stared hostilely at Novak. "Who might you be?"

Novak returned the stare.

"Doctor of Medicine, is it?"

Bikel drew himself together huffily. "Doctor of Naturopathy," he said in a chilly voice. "I happen to be attending Mrs. Boyd."

Novak glanced back and chuckled. "I'd say you got your work cut out for you. Compulsive eater, looks like. Block that thyroid."

Bikel's lips set. "You are impudent, young man. I do not like impudence. You may expect to hear from me."

"Fine," Novak said. "Mrs. Boyd can tell you where I hang out. Staying in the hotel?"

"Room 522."

"Don't run the bill too high. The Tilden's allergic to medicine men with mail order diplomas." He pushed past Bikel and down the hall. Goddamn whatever desk clerk registered Bíkel into the Tilden. The guy looked as phony as a three-dollar bill. You must eat only natural foods, dear lady. Psyllium seed is a natural aid to the elimination of bodily wastes. And your thoughts must be as pure as rainwater. Well, at least he didn't seem to be a needle man from Dream Street. To get a Narcotics license you still needed more than a claw-hammer coat, a celluloid collar and a five-buck diploma.

A sound knifed through his thoughts, halting him suddenly. Turning, he glanced down the hall and heard it again. Not from inside the Boyd suite, but not far away. Muffled by a thick door. A woman's scream.

Novak sprinted down the corridor, halting in front of 516. The room directly across from Julia Boyd's. One hand fingered the master key in his pocket as he pressed an ear against the door panel. From inside, a man's voice snarling indistinguishable words, a woman whimpering. Then the hard crack of flesh on flesh. The woman sobbed.

Novak set his jaw and thumbed the door button. He stepped slightly back from the door and his hands folded into fists. He rolled his sloping shoulders and waited.

The door opened.

A man peered out. His face was mottled, his voice unsteady. "Yeah?" he bristled.

"What seems to be the trouble?"

"Trouble?" The man laughed unpleasantly. "Wouldn't know what you're talking about. Beat it."

He made an effort to slam the door but Novak's foot blocked it. Leaning forward, Novak heaved his shoulder and the door burst inward. The man staggered back cursing.

His hair was flint-black, making his sallow skin look even paler. His upper lip sprouted a thin mustache that added some years to a handsome, weak face. His narrowed eyes were the milky-blue of hard-frozen water. He wore a shirt of sky-blue silk, cuffs peeled back.

The open collar was yoked by a black tie lightly figured with maroon darts. "What the hell…" he blurted.

"I'm Novak. Hotel Security. Where's the woman?"

To see her, all he had to do was glance sideways and down. Her back was braced against the edge of a chair, her legs folded under her thighs. She wore a filmy white dressing gown, one sleeve ripped. Her cheeks showed ugly patches of red, the rest of her face was bloodless. When she looked up, Novak saw that her eyes were wide and gray. One hand worked aimlessly through her ash blonde hair. Paula Norton's puffed lips opened and closed again.

Novak turned to Silk Shirt, snapped, "Pick her up."

The man called him something obscene. Novak took a step toward him. "This is a single room. Only the lady's registered."

Paula Norton was getting groggily to her feet.

The man stared at her and his lips formed a warped grin. "Wanna make a complaint, honey? So tell the man." He swaggered toward her.

Paula Norton wet her lips. One hand delicately touched the red patch on her right cheek. Slowly, dazedly, she said, "I fell down, that's all."

Novak blinked.

Silk Shirt guffawed. "Shove off, hero. No company wanted. Just friends here. See? Just friends." His hand darted into his pocket and pulled out a wad of folded bills. Without looking at the top one, he peeled it off and tossed it at Novak. "You made a mistake, peeper. The ten squares it. Now dust."

Novak looked down at the bill on the carpet and a slow grin twisted his lips. "I needed that," he said softly, leaned forward and slapped the man's left cheek. Hard. The man gurgled and his eyes went wild. From the hips up his body started to shake. Novak slapped the other cheek. Harder and a little lower. A drop of blood appeared on the man's upper lip. His face was scarlet now, jaw muscles working like a skein of worms. The pupils of his eyes had contracted. His tongue darted out, licked away the drop of blood. Another took its place. Suddenly he dropped his head and lunged at Novak.

Novak shifted his body to the left and took the man's head into chancery. The arms flailed wildly.

From behind him Paula Norton gasped, "Let him go."

Novak said nothing. He tightened the pressure on the man's neck until he felt the body start to sag. Then something jabbed his back just above the right kidney. Slowly his head turned and he looked around.

The pistol was a chrome-plated stocking model, no better than a .25 caliber, but pointed where it was, it could ruin a kidney or worse.

Novak shrugged, unlaced his fingers and lifted his elbow. The man fell free, crumpling onto the carpet. Novak didn't look down. He could hear gurgling sounds, the rasp of nails as fingers clawed the carpet.

Very slowly he faced her. "What the hell," he said. "We forgot to choose up sides."

Along her nose lay the silvery trails of tears. She

shook her head and bit her lips. The gun arm went limp and dropped along her thigh.

She must have been in the shower when the guy came in because the dressing gown was all she wore. The legs were nicely muscled and they melted into slim thighs. Her stomach was taut and she had never been a nursing mother. From the floor came moaning, half-formed words.

Novak rasped, "A girl like you—and a bolo like him. Baby, in case you didn't know it, he was beating you up."

Her eyes opened and for a brief instant something seemed to cloud their grayness. Then her shoulders slumped. One hand brushed hair back from her forehead. "Maybe I had it coming, Novak. Whatever happened was my affair, not yours. Leave it at that. You're well out of it. Believe me. Thanks and all that and now get the hell out."

"Jesus," Novak exploded, "if he was only playful before, now he'll be in a mood to twist your neck off."

The pistol lifted slightly. "You could call him a moody guy," she said bitterly. "Big Ben Barada. I guess there's worse."

Novak moistened dry lips, croaked, "Anything you say, Miss Norton. I'll be as far away as your phone."

"Thanks," she said and made an effort at a smile. "Everything's under control."

Novak toed the moving body. "Know him long?" he asked.

Her lips parted for a reedy laugh. "Know him? I was married to him." Suddenly she turned, her arms folded

across her waist and her shoulders began to shake
soundlessly. Novak stared at her for a moment, spun
around and strode for the door. From the hall he
slammed it shut. The things you learn about people.
The girl with the Skye terrier packed a chrome-plated
.25. Ben Barada—the name meant nothing to Novak.
Apparently somewhere it did.

In cold fury he rode the elevator down to the lobby
and jogged to his office. From the locked drawer he
pulled the Irish and drank two long gulps. Then he put
the bottle away and mopped his forehead. The neck
of his collar was limp with perspiration. Miss Paula
Norton, once Mrs. Ben Barada—whoever the hell he
was—taking a working-over from her ex-husband without a squawk. And pulling a gun on her defender. Too
screwy to figure. Like the lady said, none of your business, Novak. Relax. Get with it. Develop the long view.
Punch the timeclock and wait for retirement to roll
around. Don't mix in other peoples' brawls. Play it
smart. Pick up the hood's tenner and bow out grace-
fully like any smart cookie. Pocket hoodlum money and
let him spit in your face. Big Ben Barada...

He was starting to turn the dial combination when
the office door opened. Whirling, he saw a heavyset
man outlined in the dimness. "The office is closed," he
barked.

"Mr. Novak?" the voice inquired. "I'm Chalmers
Boyd. You were kind enough to talk with my wife and
I'd appreciate a word or two with you."

Novak ran his finger around the inside of his wet

collar. "Have a seat, Mr. Boyd." He poked the ceiling lamp button and light flared through the office.

The man who walked toward him was two inches shorter than Novak and forty pounds heavier. There was a lodge button in his coat lapel. From pockets in his double-breasted vest swung a thick-linked gold chain. On it hung a small carved ivory ball. Mr. Chalmers Boyd had a slightly receding hairline, teeth the color of dusty ivory and meaty jowls that wobbled as he walked. Settling himself ponderously in the chair, he passed one hand across his forehead and blinked at Novak. "I want this to remain confidential between us," he said in a deep voice. "Can I have your assurance on that point?"

"Sure," Novak said. "Unless breaking the law is involved."

Boyd frowned, then said officiously, "I can assure you that I am not a lawbreaker, Mr. Novak. I am a wealthy man and a man in my position cannot afford to take chances with the law. I'll have you know that my reputation is spotless."

"No need to overdo it, Mr. Boyd. I'm only the House Security man and I impress pretty easy," Novak snapped. He sat down at his desk and lighted a cigarette.

Boyd gazed at him warily, one hand closed and opened and he said, sighing, "Mrs. Boyd is in a delicate nervous condition, Mr. Novak. Brought on, no doubt, by her obesity. Orthodox medicine failed to find a cure so I consented to her consulting Dr. Bikel, whom, I gather, you met. He seems to have found means of checking her recurring hysteria. Whatever my feeling concerning his personality, I must admit that Dr. Bikel has done Julia a world of good."

Novak blew smoke at the desk lamp. It purpled, faded into gray and drifted away. "Yes," he said. "When I saw Mrs. Boyd she was as relaxed as a milch cow. And after a ninety-thousand dollar loss."

Boyd cleared his throat. His eyes flickered and he said, "That's the point I want to get across. Julia suffers frequent delusions. There was no loss of jewelry. It was never in this hotel." He coughed nervously. "Tell me, have you reported anything to the police?"

"I was leaving that to Mrs. Boyd—or you."

A smile grew until it covered Boyd's face. Like a flash flood over barren desert. Heartily he said, "Then there's no problem at all." He stood up and wiped the side of his neck. "I appreciate the tactful way you've handled the incident, Mr. Novak, and I'll be happy to write a letter of appreciation to your superiors."

"That won't be necessary," Novak said dryly. "All I did was not make a phone call." He stood up and watched Boyd walking toward the door. "If the jewelry never got to Washington, where is it now?"

Chuckling, Boyd turned as he reached for the doorknob. "Where it is always kept, Mr. Novak. In my office safe. In Winnetka, Illinois."

Then the door opened and Mr. Chalmers Boyd went out. The Big Noise from Winnetka. Novak stepped back, opened a section of the window and sniffed cold night air. For all his money Mr. Chalmers Boyd needed to see a dentist. He had a breath like a polecat.

After a while Novak moved to his file safe and

twirled the dial combination. He opened a drawer filled with 3 x 5 cards and thumbed them expertly. When he found the name he was looking for, he pulled the card and studied the typed notations. Then he returned it, locked the safe and walked out.

3

Pausing at the end of the reception counter, Novak beckoned the clerk over. "Percy," he said, "I checked that 515 complaint and it was baseless. No loss, no robbery. Not even any jewelry. According to Mr. Boyd it's safe in his office in Winnetka. Just a woman with high blood pressure and occasional delusions. So let's not be hollering for me every time a waiter loses a napkin, eh, Perce? And another thing. In this business you got to be able to screen a phony from the real article."

The clerk said nothing.

Novak said, "I'm talking about the herb doctor you booked into 522, Percy."

The clerk snorted, consulted a registration card and twittered, "Dr. Bikel's bill is being taken care of by the Boyds. So there."

Novak's teeth made a sucking sound. "Sorry, Perce," he muttered and angled over toward the newsstand. He bought a pack of cigarettes from the cutie behind the counter and lighted one. She laid her arms on the counter and put her weight on them. The strain pushed her breasts up and she gave Novak a thoughtful stare. "Working kind of late tonight, Pete," she murmured.

"Tonight and every night."

"My name's Sylvia, you know."

"Yep. I got your card on file. Sylvia Riordan. Age:

twenty-six, divorced. Got a kid in school. Education: secretarial school. Plays house with a couple of regular customers."

"Gumshoe," she hissed. "Remind me to slit your throat some dark night in Lafayette Park."

"There's a line of volunteers ahead of you, gorgeous. Anyway, your next night off give me a growl. We could sip a glass of schnapps up at my place. One thing could lead to another."

"Sorry," she snapped. "I seem to have lost interest."

His face looked pained. "Did I say something? About the middle-aged boyfriends? Hell, I'm the last guy in the world to get jealous."

She had turned away to arrange paperback books in a rack. Glancing back she said, "You don't kid me, Pete. Anyone cheating on you you'd tear apart with your teeth."

He felt his face stiffen. "Don't make any bets on that. The fires of youth are long since damped. What does sentiment get you? An empty coffee cup and a stained spoon." Reaching across the counter he patted her cheek lightly. "Sorry, sweetie. Bad mood tonight."

"What happened? Trouble with the manager again?"

"That bottom-pincher?" He shook his head. "A girl," he said softly. "A girl getting slammed around by a heel who shouldn't even be in the same city with her. And she boosted for him." He let smoke spiral out from his nostrils. "You could say it piqued me a little. See you, Sylvia." He moved along the lobby wall, turned into the men's bar and saw the usual crowd of well-dressed gonifs and five-percenters selling each other chunks of

Capitol Hill carved from the air, with arm gestures made uneven by expense account vodka marts and rye on the rocks. Over the bar hung a light haze of tobacco smoke. Conditioner not working too well. Fred, the head bartender, with a face lined like Lincoln's and white hair as light and carefully brushed as a baby's. Hi, Freddie, Novak mouthed silently and passed along.

From the second ballroom the muffled beat of a dance orchestra. What was it tonight? The Owls? The Odd Fellows? No, let's rack that honeycomb brain, Novak. Got it: Gamma Tau Sorority's spring bash. The Gamma Tau lasses were from a night secretarial school. Their beaus would be working stiffs in rented tuxes and stiff-bosomed shirts the wrong size. Play on, wild strings, play on.

In the florist shop only a window light. The airline reservation stand in the corner was dark. The Western Union counter held a yellow sign with a black arrow pointing at a nearby telephone. The sightseeing booth was empty, the top littered with giveaway folders: See Colonial Williamsburg. Four-Hour Tour of the Nation's Capital, Chinatown Included. Visit Historic Mount Vernon. Sail to Relaxing Virginia Beach. Moonlight Cruise on the Potomac River. See… Do…Visit…Ride… Lord, can't anyone sit down and think any more? Without turning on the silver tube? Or read a book that isn't condensed from the Original (unexpurgated) Version?

Wearily, Novak slid into an upholstered chair and butted his cigarette in the sandy stand. Off in one corner an old man in a gray whipcord uniform was sifting butt stands and stamping HT on the smooth surface. Wiry white hair and a face like worn cordovan. Shuffling along in toeless shoes, carrying the sieve and trash bucket. Novak closed his eyes and massaged them with his fingers. A long day. Too much to do, not enough time to think. Ought to go home and hit the pad. Tune the FM to a little Brahms and soothe the aching cortex. Relax until the alarm breaks you out. All quiet at the Tilden.

Except for the obese wife of a wealthy industrialist, the furtive face of a raw food quack and the memory of a silk-shirted hoodlum tossing a green bill on the carpet for you to crawl and fetch.

All quiet except for the tortured face of a gray-eyed, ash blonde lovely with a showgirl's body and a conscience heavier than a carload of sins. Mouth, a slash of red; eyes that pleaded for pity, understanding. And lips that told nothing....

Novak opened his eyes, blinked away whirling circles and stretched his legs stiffly. Shoes needing a shine. Tomorrow in his room would do. Pick up clean shirts from the Chinaman's. Buy a bottle of sauce before the package stores closed. Tomorrow he had things to do, places to go. A few hours in the kip was the sensible prescription.

Novak got up slowly and eased himself across the lobby. He slid behind the reception counter and thumbed through the registration file. Dr. Edward Bikel. From Antelope Wells, N.M. A glance at Room 522's mailbox told him both keys were there and Bikel was out. For dinner, probably, and a night on the town.

If the doc were still cosseting Julia Boyd he'd have one key in his pocket.

Novak went over to the elevators and rode one to the fifth floor. The doors slid apart and Novak brushed past a young couple waiting to ride down. The man had on a dinner jacket and a plaid tie. The girl wore a willow-green dress with a net stole and an orchid corsage. Honeymooners, most likely. May it last forever, he thought as he turned down the corridor.

The make-up maid was wheeling her change cart toward him. As he passed she said, "Everything quiet up here, Mr. Novak."

"That's how it ought to be. I'll be in 522 a few minutes, Anna. If the guy comes back, stall him, huh?"

"If I see him."

Novak stopped and turned. "A single in 516, checked in before seven o'clock. Looks like dough but keep her in mind. Anything out of line, let me know."

"S'what I'm supposed to do. A looker?"

"She wiggles when she walks."

Anna snorted, bent over to rub one kneecap and trudged on, pushing her cart with its carefully hung towels, bathmats and trays of hotel soap, sterile glasses and washcloths.

Novak reached 522 soundlessly, pressed his ear to the door panel and palmed the knob slowly. Locked. No sound from inside. Glancing down the corridor he slipped the master key in the lock, turned the handle and went in. Slipping the safety bolt he turned on the ceiling light.

On the luggage rack a Gladstone bag. Beneath it a

pair of black shoes with elastic inserts instead of laces. A tidy person, Dr. Bikel. In the closet hung a dark poplin raincoat and a black pinchtop hat. Nothing more. The bathroom cabinet held a worn, ivory-handled straight razor and a scraggly pigbristle brush. There was a toothbrush with *Northwest Airlines* stamped along the handle, souvenir of an overnight flight sometime in the not recent past. Beside it a small plastic box of salt. Use only natural products. Heh, heh.

Novak went back to the luggage rack. The Gladstone was locked, but a minute's labor with a spring-steel pick solved it. Opening the bag, Novak straightened it on the rack and untied the interior ribbons.

There were three white shirts, two dark ties, several pairs of black silk socks and some striped underwear. Novak lifted the divider and examined the other side.

There was a dark worsted suit and a roll of *Natural Health* magazines. He poked the suit and felt something hard under the folds of the coat. Lifting it out he saw a brown medicinal bottle with no label on it. He unscrewed the top and sniffed.

The scent was pepsin mixed with cherry. Carrying the bottle to the bathroom he tilted it at the washbowl and saw pinkish syrup roll out. He dabbed one finger and touched it to the end of his tongue. The syrup had a pleasant taste—of pepsin and cherry flavoring. The doctor's medicine, or Julia Boyd's?

He screwed the cap back on the bottle and replaced it in the folds of the coat. Funny Bikel wouldn't have hung up the suit when he checked in. Most travelers did. And once inside their room they usually left their bags unlocked. Not so Bikel. The bottle wasn't meant to be seen. Novak wondered why.

As he smoothed the suit and retied the retaining ribbons the phone began to ring. The sound halted his hands. He straightened and stared at the telephone. It rang four more times, then stopped. Novak sucked in a deep breath and closed the Gladstone, locking it with his spring-steel pick. Then he went over to the writing table.

On the blotter lay a Western Union telegram pad. Tilting it toward the light he could see scrawled impressions from the previous sheet. All he could make out was that the telegram had been sent to Chicago, signed Ed. Not much to go on there. He picked up the telephone and called the desk. When Percy answered, Novak said, "This medicine man Bikel—when did he check in?"

"Two days ago."

"And the Chalmers Boyds?"

"Same date."

Novak fished a cigarette from his pocket, lighted it with one hand and blew smoke at the writing desk. "What's Boyd in town for?"

"There's a convention of Building and Loan Association presidents. I've seen him wearing a blue badge with his name on it."

"That's pretty clever," Novak conceded. "Mrs. Boyd go out much?"

"I saw her cross the lobby earlier this evening—just

before she called about her jewelry. Other than that no." He tittered. "Must take a power of calories to move bulk like hers."

"Yeah. And all from raw carrots." He hung up, wiped his prints from the phone out of habit and crossed to the door. From the hallway no sound. Novak opened the catch and slipped out. At the end of the corridor Anna was gathering things from her wagon and carrying them into an open doorway. When she saw Novak she waved all-clear.

He walked on down the corridor, passed 516, slowed and turned back. Cupping the cigarette in his hand he took a long drag and let the smoke filter out of his nostrils. Maybe Ben Barada was still there, maybe not. Why *Big* Ben? Hell, he was only five-ten, a hundred sixty, a pushover in a light breeze. Novak's hand slid up along his tie, adjusted the knot, patted his lapels and settled on the door button. He jabbed it, heard the distant response and waited. No soft footsteps padding toward the door. No lilting female query. Novak poked the button savagely. Still no response.

Stepping back he looked up and down the corridor. Anna was out of sight in the make-up room. Novak pulled the master key from his pocket and fitted it into the lock. Opening it quickly he stepped inside.

The room was lighted. It was also occupied.

Paula Norton was sitting up on the sofa. Light glinted from the chrome-plated gun in her right hand. As Novak elbowed the door shut he heard breath whistle between her teeth. The gun arm dropped listlessly and she lay back. Coolly, she said, "Mandrake the Magician.

He goes through doors, walks on ceilings. Now you see him, now you don't." One hand fumbled for an ice pack beside her thigh, lifted it against the side of her face. Her eyes closed. "You're crowding your luck a little, Novak. Anyone but you and I might have pressed the trigger. I'm that jittery tonight."

"Don't tell me why," Novak said and walked toward her. "Let's keep it a big secret, take our lumps and suffer in silence." He reached down, picked up the pistol and extracted the magazine. Seven copper-point slugs plus one in the chamber. He slid the magazine back and flicked the safety on. Then he laid the pistol on the coffee table. "You weren't kidding," he said thoughtfully.

A short laugh answered him. "The crowd I played with used blanks once a year, Novak—on the Fourth of July."

"Barada's crowd?"

One hand shifted the ice pack to the other side of her face. Novak sat down at the end of the sofa and lifted her feet across his lap. He pulled off her slippers and began massaging the arch of one foot.

"Hey," she called, "that tickles, you oaf."

Novak grinned. "Endure it, beautiful. It's a great relaxer. A hockey trainer taught me about feet." His strong fingers kept up a regular pulsating pressure and when he felt the tenseness leave her leg he shifted to the other foot.

After a while Paula said, "Okay, coach, why the subtle entrance with the master key?"

Novak shrugged. "Last time I came in you were on

the floor. I wondered where you'd be this time."

"With my face the way it is, you knew I'd be here."

"Yeah. But alive or dead—that was the question."

She turned on one side, facing the back of the sofa. "You came at a good time at that," she said huskily. "God knows what he'd have done if you hadn't come when you did."

Novak slid the slippers back on her feet and straightened the crease in his trousers. "By then you'd taken your beating," he said. "Why stop me from slapping him around a little?"

"Maybe I found myself liking you. Guys who slap Ben Barada around don't live long enough to tell the story in the corner saloon."

"Yeah," he said. "Barada copped five spaces at Joliet. The right contacts got him out early on clemency and a floating parole. Armed robbery."

"Ben's a gambler," she said tunelessly. "He drifted into a brace game in Moline, it was a packed deal. Afterward Ben came back for his money. Someone called the cops." She turned around and sat up. "I thought you never heard of Ben."

"I've done some research, sweetheart, but there wasn't anything on you. Want to tell me?"

She looked at him for a long time. Then she said, "What for, Novak? I'm checking out tomorrow. You'll never see me again."

"Friends call me Pete," he said cheerfully. "Let's say it's for the record—my files. The story of Mrs. Ben Barada."

"Why?"

He shrugged. "It's a lonely life around the Tilden. Other guys with a wife and a TV set go home. Me—I got my files. For those long winter nights."

She gave him a thin smile. "We were married—you know that. I was a hoofer doing a specialty in a Jackson Park spot when I met Ben. We got along pretty good— he shaved anyway, and he dressed well. I guess I don't have to tell you what the hoofer's grind is like, doing the four-and-dirty bit. Sure, my legs don't look too much like tree stumps and I've got a good body but so have ten thousand other shuckers. And no Hollywood agent ever propositioned me." She breathed deeply. "Ben did. And he added a ring." One hand opened slowly. "We made out for a while, then he got sent to Joliet for five years." She leaned forward. "In Illinois a felony sentence is grounds for divorce. I waited a year, two years. Then I met a man. He took me out, sent expensive presents, but that was all. Finally he hired a lawyer and arranged the divorce."

One hand lifted, her teeth sank into a knuckle. "I didn't know Ben would get clemency. Three months ago he walked out. By then I'd had enough of the other guy, but Ben heard about him."

"So he came here to beat you up."

"Ben wanted a stake," she said dully. "He figured I'd saved a pile from...from the guy. Well, I hadn't. Life's short, Pete. Why stick your green in a clay pig and watch life slip by?" One hand ran through her ash blonde hair. "I've got an apartment in Chicago, a car and the clothes on my back. Nothing more."

Novak reached up and covered her right hand. It

felt smooth and cool against his palm. "I don't much care for the divorce part," he said quietly, "but twisting your arm for money is worse. What made him think you had any?"

"I told him so. I told him I was collecting it here. In Washington."

"Have you?"

"Not yet." Her hand drew away from his. "If you didn't like the other part, you'll like this even less: I'm here for a shakedown, Novak. I've got something a guy wants. Something he has to pay for. A hunk of dough." Her eyes found his and her chin lifted aggressively.

"How much?" Novak asked.

"Ninety grand."

4

"Ninety grand," Novak murmured and got up. From his coat he pulled a fresh cigarette, offered it to her. She shook her head.

Novak lighted the cigarette, dropped the lighter into his pocket. "That ought to keep Ben Barada in green baize for quite a while."

Her eyes lifted slowly. "You don't know Ben. All right, you've heard the Norton story. You asked for it. Any comment?"

Novak peered around the room. "Any whisky handy?"

"There's a pint in the bedroom."

He walked away from her, turned on the bedroom light and carried the pint into the bathroom. He broke the seals on two glasses, poured amber fluid into them and added ice cold water from the tap. He carried the drinks back to the sofa and handed one to her.

She brushed hair from her forehead and tossed off the drink. Novak sipped his slowly. She lowered the empty glass to the carpet. "I said any comments?"

"A couple. First, I think maybe you earned a poke on the jaw for the felony divorce. But nothing more. Second, you don't owe Ben Barada ninety grand or any part of it. Third, I think I know where the dough's coming from, and fourth, I'd forget about it if I were you."

Her eyes had widened. "Why?"

"A shakedown's equivalent to blackmail, sweetie, and this is federal territory. They don't just let you off with a lecture and a slap on the wrist. They hang the book on you. It's a federal rap and the payoff takes years. Why?" He leaned over, his face a foot from hers. "Because the game you're playing is the sort of thing every Senator and Congressman is scared to death some hustler will pull on him. I'm not moralizing, beautiful. I'm telling you hard facts. If you're going through with it, run, do not walk, from the District of Columbia. Try Baltimore or Delaware. The officials there are elected, not appointed, and there's less flint in their stare. You'd stand a better chance of having something to show for your trouble." He lifted his glass, drank again. "But if you're doing it just so Barada can line his wallet you're dumber than I think."

Her face went white around the eyes. "I gave up charity when I quit the Brownies," she said stonily. "Ben said he'd kill me if I didn't come through."

Novak laughed shortly. "I've seen this would-be killer and even his eyeballs are yellow." He shook his head. "Don't fall for it. You paid him off tonight when you poked your gun in my ribs. Next time he comes around talking tough, shove it in his."

Her face turned away, her eyes closed and her breasts rose and fell. After a while her eyes opened and she said quietly, "I haven't had a pep talk in quite a while, coach. I'll think it over."

Novak finished his drink and put down the glass beside the chromed pistol. He stared at it speculatively. The girl got up slowly, drew the dressing gown around her body and came to him. Her hands met behind his neck. "Novak," she murmured. "What's that, Hungarian?"

"Central Europe, anyway. The part that used to change names every two generations. How about Norton? Sounds English but you don't look it."

Her nose wrinkled. "A booking agent's idea. If I don't look it it's because one grandmother was a full-blooded Osage. The family always called her a princess, but you know families. Oklahoma families, anyway."

Her lips were a fraction of an inch away. Novak closed the gap, kissing the bruised lips lightly. Her body clung to his, her hand was doing something with the hair behind his head. Her eyelids fluttered and closed. Her tongue darted into his mouth, searched and withdrew. Under his hand the flesh of her back quivered like the flanks of a nervous filly. Finally she drew away and stared at him. "You're all man," she breathed. "As if I didn't know."

"Like Chinese food?"

"Uh huh."

"I know a place on H Street that's open all night."

"And me looking the way I do?"

"We can char a cork and go blackface."

Paula giggled.

Just then the telephone shrilled. Gaiety drained from her face and her body tensed. Novak growled, "I'll take it."

"No." One hand held him. She moved away toward the phone. Novak ran one hand through his rumpled hair and watched her pick up the receiver. "Yes?" she said tautly.

As she listened her face hardened. Finally the rasp of the other voice stopped and she said, "I haven't made up my mind. I'll let you know tomorrow." The other voice said something. She said, "No, nothing definite. I'll get in touch with you. Yes—before noon. All right."

The receiver clicked down hard and she turned back to Novak.

"The psychological moment," she said thinly. "Thanks for the dinner invitation, but it will have to be another night."

"You're leaving tomorrow."

"Am I?" She laughed brittlely. "Yes, I'd forgotten that. Well, I'll write you a letter."

"You and every other girl," he said, turned and strode toward the door. When he looked back she was sitting on the sofa, her face toward the wall.

"Keep the payoff in small bills," he rasped. "Banks record anything bigger than a yard."

Opening the door, he went out.

No Ben Barada lurking in the corridor. No Doc Bikel slinking down the hall. It must have been the mark calling Paula, not her ex-husband. She'd said she hadn't made up her mind yet, that she wasn't sure. But she'd go through with it. A dame gets a case of conscience and nothing can shrive her. The shucker and the big-time gambler. He could see her in the smoky arc of a purple spot, rolling her hips, flipping her rouged nipples, bumping and grinding, socking it at the wet-lipped customers—and hating it.

As Novak walked along the corridor he remembered the warm, sensual pressure of her nearly naked body, the hotness of her mouth, the tilt of her breasts and the taper of her thighs. He swallowed hard, stopped in front of the elevator doors and punched the Down button savagely. Ben Barada's ex-wife and still his girl.

He rode the elevator moodily to the lobby and made his way through a noisy crowd of new arrivals waiting to register.

K Street was cool, the sidewalk slick with condensed moisture. A silver Alfa Romeo shot past, glowing like the tail of a comet. The big money. You got it any way you could and thumbed your nose at the peasants. Conspicuous Consumption, Veblen had called it. Like Mrs. Julia Boyd's ninety-thousand dollar loss that didn't even ruffle a hair.

Novak pushed through a doorway, slid his frame onto a bar stool and scraped a dollar bill from his pocket. The bartender moved over to him. "What'll it be, Pete? The usual?"

"Yeah, Irish." He shook out a cigarette, lighted it and looked around. Names changed but never the faces. The lush at the far end of the bar gravely building unsuccessful houses from glossy match folders. The hatless woman in the booth, strained white face and an ashtray heaped with half-smoked cigarettes; waiting for a man to come. The kid staring at her from the bar stool, working up enough whisky courage to go over and slide into the booth beside her. Lonely people. Washington was full of them. Government workers, clerks, stenos and middle-grade bureaucrats. A town of anonymous, rootless people. Transients. The only city in the U.S. permanently dedicated to sightseeing and conventions. L'Enfant's town, designed after Paris, with streets converging at circles where grapeshot gunners could make a clean sweep.

He sipped his drink, stared at the TV screen on a ledge above the bottle shelves, watched a comedian getting a big laugh from a studio audience by wearing a funnel for a hat and a hula skirt over his shorts. Heap big fun, Novak thought, and finished his drink.

The bartender came over and lifted the empty glass. "Do it again?"

"Not tonight, Alex." He slid off the stool and took a deep breath. "I'm for the pads."

Alex ironed the dollar bill between two fingers and said, "Don't feel too good myself. Change of seasons, maybe. Cool and wet, air's too heavy."

"Yeah. One of those nights you think you got to chew your way home."

Alex nodded.

Novak gave him a crooked grin, then headed for the door. He had a car but he garaged it near his apartment four blocks away. He walked up Seventeenth Street, crossed and turned at N. The elms were heavy with spring leaves, obscuring the sidewalk light from street lamps. Set back from the walk were graystone houses with spiral steps and barred basement windows. Once a fashionable residential neighborhood, the area was now given over largely to rooming houses. A few of the larger ones had been divided into three and four apartments. This year Novak lived in one of them.

The entrance to his apartment stairway was down what had been a service alley in the era when the owner had been able to afford servants. Now it was only a narrow concrete access-way with a garage door at the far end, tree-laden and dark.

There were two concrete risers to the doorway. Novak stepped up and felt in his pocket for the key.

At that moment arms circled him and tightened.

He jerked up his legs putting all his weight on the other's arms. He heard a grunt. Then he stamped the man's arches viciously and heard a breathy yelp. The pinioning arms burst apart and Novak lurched free. He was grabbing for his shoulder holster when another shape came at him from the side. The cosh smashed his right shoulder and the arm went numb. As he spun around, the first man tried to tackle him. Novak's knee crunched into his attacker's face. The body dropped aside, rolling, white hands clawing at a bubbling nose.

He had lost track of the other man. His left hand fumbled for the .38 but things were happening too fast. From behind him the cosh made a fast purring sound and the back of Novak's head exploded. As he dropped forward he managed to spin sideways, protecting his face. He felt the impact distantly. His world filled with spinning lights. Something was thudding into his ribs with the relentless power of rubber mallets. A voice shrilled, "Jesus, Tags, Ben didn't say kill him!"

Then darkness.

5

He floated in astral darkness, feeling the lifeless cold of outer space, hearing the brittle chiming of icy bells. He drifted back slowly; gray haze formed, whirled like windblown fog and threaded away. Pain blew its paralyzing breath through his mouth, giggled and chipped at his frozen brain.

Groaning he rolled over and opened his eyes.

The darkness stayed silent. He was alone.

His right arm felt like splintered ice. He sat up slowly, groped for his revolver, felt its bulk and tried to get up. The effort made him gnaw his lip; pointed shoes had kicked his ribs. The bruises were like ripe boils.

Using his left hand he levered himself off the pavement to his knees, then staggered upright. In the distance the honk of a lonely horn. No sound of running feet. The heavies were long gone.

Leaning against the doorway he studied the dial of his watch and tried to focus his mind. Unless he had walked more slowly than usual he had been unconscious nearly a quarter of an hour.

He could hardly lift his hand to fit the key into the lock.

Door open, he felt for the light switch and saw the staircase materialize before him like a slide thrown on a wall. His head throbbed like a deep Brazilian drum.

Half pulling himself with his left arm, he made it to the top of the stairs, found the key to his apartment door and opened it.

He tottered into the room, pulling off his coat, loosening the leather shoulder strap and opening his collar. The revolver dropped to the sofa and he angled dizzily toward the bathroom.

No marks on his face. He leaned against the washbasin and unbuttoned his shirt with the fingers of his left hand, cursing their clumsiness.

Blue-black welts marred his chest. His back ached. The way his right shoulder looked he was lucky the cosh hadn't snapped the collarbone. Turning, he ran hot water into the tub, stripped and swallowed two codeine tablets.

The bathwater was so hot he could barely stand it. Wincing, he entered it slowly and when it covered him entirely he closed his eyes and felt a wave of nausea surge over him. Shock and pain, old friends, both. His lips twisted and then the codeine began to take hold.

He opened his eyes and studied a bruise on his left thigh. The hoods had done their work well, but he had given one of them a bloody souvenir. Barada's boys. Cheap alley muggers. One named Tags. Just a warning this time, no knife at the gullet, no throttle-cord tightening around the throat. He smiled grimly. Lucky I didn't really get Barada mad at me.

His left hand massaged his right shoulder tenderly. The pain was bearable. He'd caught plenty of slashing hockey sticks on both arms, how many years ago was it? No trainer now to bake out the pain and strap his ribs. Maybe Doc Bikel would know a remedy. Possibly a dram of cherry-pepsin syrup from an unlabeled brown bottle. Not a natural substance, Doc. Smelled highly artificial. Don't let the Nature brotherhood know, they might call it unethical.

In the living room the telephone rasped. Novak felt his scalp hairs rise. It buzzed again like a rattler under a forked stick. Barada probably. Yeah, Barada. Calling to hiss out another warning. Well, pal, I read you loud and clear. I get the message.

Shivering, he closed his eyes.

After a while the phone stopped ringing.

The back of his head was sticky with drying blood. He cleaned it off slowly and threw the streaked washcloth into the corner. Drying himself slowly, he felt giddiness return and steadied himself against the wall. Then he pulled on pajama bottoms and staggered off to bed.

The next time the phone rang the clock showed nearly one o'clock. He awoke stiffly, reached for the receiver, then drew back his hand. Barada again, or one of his boys. Why give them the satisfaction of jeering at him?

He rolled over and tried to forget the telephone but it shrilled insistently. Finally he grabbed it and snarled, "Novak here, what'll it be?"

The voice that replied was reedy with terror. Paula Norton's voice. "Pete—I...I called before. Something's happened."

"Well, Mrs. Barada, I'm scarcely answering the phone these days—the effort's so painful."

"Pain?…Pete, what's the matter?"

"Oh, nothing mortal. Your ex-husband sent around a couple of muscle boys to kick my teeth out. All they did was cave my ribs."

Her throat made a sucking gasp.

Novak said, "Let's not talk about my little problems; alongside yours they're probably trivial."

Her voice came back, pitched a little lower. "I have no right to ask you anything—I know that. But I'm in trouble. Bad trouble, Pete."

He sat up slowly. Along his spine the skin was icy. "You wouldn't want to talk about it over the phone."

"No."

"And it can't wait until morning? I could use a—"

"I'm sorry, I shouldn't have called. No, it can't wait until morning. By then you'll have to talk with me through bars."

He wiped sweat from his upper lip. "Mix yourself a drink," he said levelly. "Mix another for me. I'm on my way."

The receiver clattered into place, the ceiling light flared on and Novak pried himself off the bed. Dressing took a long time; when he bent over to pull on his shoes the effort made his temples pound painfully.

Finally he was dressed. He strapped on the shoulder holster and walked down the stairway.

Opening the garage doors took more effort. Setting his teeth he told himself he should have downed another pain pill. Then he was backing the Pontiac out of the alley, driving down Seventeenth toward the Tilden.

He found a parking place two blocks away and went

in by the service entrance. No one paid any attention to him as he slipped into the room service elevator and punched the UP button.

Leaning in one corner he closed his eyes and sucked deep breaths to steady himself. The elevator hummed to a gentle stop at the fifth floor.

Novak stepped out. The doors closed behind him.

Before he turned into the corridor he listened for voices and footsteps but the floor was silent. Even so he moved quietly along the wall until he was at her door. Touching the buzzer lightly he opened the door with the master key and closed it behind him.

She was sitting in an upholstered chair, wearing black toreador pants and an indigo blouse with puffed sleeves. Her knees were drawn up and held by laced fingers. Her eyes had a vacant, brooding look. Below them her cheekbones were as white as ivory.

As he walked toward her she said, "I didn't mix your drink. Ever since I called you I've been sitting here as if I were frozen." Her eyelids fluttered and her hands released her knees.

"The drinks can wait. Tell me what you couldn't over the phone."

Her eyebrows raised and she began to giggle. The tone was false, rising. Her shoulders shook.

"Stop it!" he snapped.

She moved her head helplessly as an ugly guffaw racked her throat. Novak slapped her face. The crack was like a pistol shot.

Shocked eyes stared up at him. Her face had gone rigid but the hysteria had drained away.

Blinking, she drew one hand across her forehead and said, "I needed that. God, I'm a softy."

He sat slowly on the sofa, a yard from her, and waited.

Her breasts lifted, her head drew back and she said, "After you left I felt lousy. No one's talked to me about right and wrong in so long I'd forgotten there was a difference. Then you walked out on me."

"It seemed like the thing to do."

She nodded slowly. "I let you go—a big mistake. How big you'll find out. Anyway, I called you and when you didn't answer I couldn't stand being cooped up here with my conscience and the four walls. I decided to go out for a walk. I looked up the vet's address and went over there—to see Toby, I told myself, but it was really to get away. Do some thinking." In the hollow of her throat a nerve fluttered lightly. Her tongue darted out, moistened her lips. "I don't know how long I walked—an hour maybe—and when I came back here I had company."

"Barada?"

One hand gestured at the dark bedroom doorway. "In there."

Novak levered himself off the sofa and trudged to the doorway. He groped for the wall switch, pressed it. White light flooded the room.

There was a mirrored dressing table, a jade-green bureau, a stool, a laden luggage rack, two chairs and twin beds. One of them had been turned back, exposing the pillow and the undersheet. The other bed had a jade green cover with white piping.

On it lay a man.

His eyes stared at the ceiling light as though they had never seen. His mouth was open but it would never speak. His arms lay slackly alongside his large body, the empty hands slightly curled. Light glinted from buffed nails.

Across his dark vest lay a golden chain, a charm of carved ivory. The cheeks of the once-hearty face had a waxy, caved-in look.

Novak moved closer.

The hair was rumpled. In the dark material of Chalmers Boyd's vest was a small hole, the edges singed black, close enough to the heart to have been instantly fatal. Novak lifted the left arm and flexed it. Then he turned the body over. No exit hole in Boyd's back. A low-power weapon. Possibly as low-caliber as a .25 pistol.

He let the body roll onto its back again. Turning off the light he went back to the girl.

"The Big Noise from Winnetka," he said hoarsely. "It's been a day full of surprises. Let's see your pistol."

She got up unsteadily, walked to the writing desk and brought back a cloth-covered purse. Opening it, she held it toward Novak.

He covered his hand with a handkerchief and lifted out the chrome-plated pistol. Removing the magazine he ejected the chamber cartridge and sniffed the muzzle. Then he tilted it toward the light and peered down the barrel. It was dusty; months probably since it had been fired. Novak bent over, cringed, picked up the cartridge and dropped it in his pocket. Then he slid the magazine into the butt, locked it and put the pistol in his pocket. Her eyes questioned him.

"Some towns you don't need a license to carry an iron," he said. "This is one where you do. I'll take that drink now."

The bottle was where he had left it. He built two strong ones and carried one over to where she was standing. "Don't just sip it," he said. "Belt it down."

As she tilted the glass Novak eased himself into a chair and fished out a cigarette. Before lighting it, he emptied his glass and set it down. "Mr. Chalmers Boyd," he said musingly. "He was going to write me a letter of commendation. Too late now." He sighed.

Her eyes glinted like pellets of ice. "So you knew him," she said tautly.

"Enough to figure him for the mark you were putting the bite on."

She nodded slowly, made her way to the sofa and sat down. Her hands opened and closed emptily.

"Maybe it wasn't Big Ben who called when I was here. Maybe it was Mr. Boyd."

"It was Boyd," she said wearily. "He wanted the jewels tonight. But I'd better tell you about that. Could you spare a cigarette?"

He lighted one for her, reached over and placed it between unsteady fingers. She sucked at it deeply, her cheeks hollowing. Gray smoke drifted toward the ceiling. "Boyd was the man I met while Ben was in Joliet," she said in an uneven voice. "I'm not particularly proud of him but he did well by me. Before we broke it off he gave me some jewelry: a sapphire ring, a diamond bracelet and an emerald brooch. He told me they were insured for ninety grand. He didn't tell me they were his wife's. That came later—when he wanted them back. By then Ben had seen them, wanted me to sell them. I told him I couldn't...that all Boyd had to do was put in a robbery beef and the jewels would be traced back to me." She drew in on the cigarette and the end glowed hotly. "So I told Boyd he could have them back for their insured price. He had to come here for his convention and we arranged to stay in the same hotel. Ben knew the arrangement, and showed up too—in case I changed my mind." Her lips twisted bitterly. "You saw how he was bucking up my morale. Well, I was ready to go through with it until we talked earlier this evening. A girl like me takes what she can get and shoves off. Thinking's too much trouble. But something changed me. Maybe the beating-up Ben gave me, maybe talking with you. Anyway, when Chalmers called me I was undecided. I thought about it after you left and then I called you. Nobody answered."

"I figured it was Barada."

"Then I went out, took my walk and came back." Her head turned slightly. "That's what I found."

"Cold company," Novak said.

Paula Norton shivered. "I couldn't bring myself to touch him. The way his eyes stared at the ceiling told me all I needed to know. What are you going to do now? Call the police?"

Novak said nothing.

Her hands knotted. "They'll hang me. They'll find out I was his fancy woman and claim I killed him. They'll never give me a chance."

"It's not as simple as that," Novak said and stood up. "The law has to prove motive, opportunity and intent. Boyd was shot through the heart—but not by your little toy. He could have been shot anywhere—there's no exit wound, no blood on your bed." His cigarette tasted like wet straw. He butted it and stared at her. "You mentioned some jewelry. Let's have a look at it."

She got up dumbly and walked into the bathroom, her slippers making little scuffling noises on the carpet. The light went on and in a moment she brought back a small bag of watered silk with a drawstring. "I keep it with my makeup," she said and opened the drawstring. As she peered into it her face went blank. Frantically one hand scrabbled around the inside and came out empty.

"They're gone!" she shrilled and threw the little bag at the sofa. Then she covered her face with her hands and sobbed. Novak watched her from his chair. She drew a small handkerchief from the slash pocket of her slacks and dabbed at her cheeks. When she could speak she said, "Ben did it, the bastard. He shot Chalmers and stole the jewels!"

"Sit down, sweetheart. We may have to do a little thinking."

As she obeyed, her eyes narrowed. "A *little* thinking? A hell of a *lot* of thinking, I'd say."

"My skull's a little battered. I don't know how much sense we can squeeze out of it." He leaned foward. "What you don't know is that Julia Boyd—your late friend's overweight widow—reported her jewels missing earlier this evening. I listened to her story and told her to report it to the police. I was barely back in my office when her husband rushed in to tell me it was all a big mistake—the jewels were back in his office safe in Winnetka. Boyd added that his wife suffered delusions and hysteria. He told me what I had already learned—that she was being treated by an herb doctor named Bikel who checked in here with the Boyds. So when you told me what you planned to do it didn't take integral calculus to identify Boyd as the turkey and the jewels as the ones his wife had reported missing." He leaned back and stared down at her white face. "Maybe Julia Boyd really thought she'd brought the jewels to Washington. People with mental twists have far crazier ideas. On the other hand, maybe she knew damn well the jewels were in the hotel. I haven't talked with her since Boyd cooled me, but it occurs to me that if she had any idea that her husband's sweetie had her jewelry, she might very well have taken wifely steps to protect her own interests: report them as stolen—nullifying their use to you, and enabling her to collect their insured value. Or maybe she'd come to some sort of an understanding with her husband—get the jewelry back from you at any cost." He wiped his lips with the back of his hand. "How much did Julia Boyd know?"

"He never mentioned her."

"Fastidious, huh? That fits." He got up heavily. "Well, the sparklers are gone. What we've got in exchange is a body. I don't like cleaning up after Ben Barada but I can't see any other way."

Her eyes had widened. There was a little color in her cheeks. Enough to show the flesh was alive.

"Hotel work," he muttered and blew a soft raspberry.

Turning, he left her and went out of the door, locking it behind him. He crossed the corridor quietly and listened in front of 515. The widow Boyd. Tomorrow would be a big test for Dr. Bikel.

Silently he slipped the key in the lock and entered. The room was totally dark. He took out his pencil flash and played it around. The furniture hadn't moved. On tiptoes he moved toward the bedroom doorway and heard a guttural snore. Good. The widow was asleep. Retracing his steps he left the room, crossed the corridor and unlocked the girl's door. She was sitting where he had left her, eyes remote, body shrunken. He went to the bedroom, bent over and tried to lift Boyd's body from the bed. The effort dizzied him and his bruised ribs slashed razors of pain through his body. His right arm was next to useless. Wincing, he lowered the dead weight and went back to where Paula was sitting. "Too heavy," he rasped. "When a guy's over forty he ought to watch his weight."

He left the room again, went down the corridor to the service closet and opened it. Propped against the wall was a dolly for heavy luggage. He wheeled it out, closed the door and pushed it back to 516 and into the bedroom. By the time he had lifted and pushed Boyd's body onto it his face was strained and he was gasping from the pain of tortured muscles. To Paula he called, "Here we come, beautiful," and began wheeling the body out of the bedroom. Glancing toward her he saw that she had turned away.

At the doorway he waited, listening, and then he pushed the dolly quickly across the corridor. Behind him Paula's door snapped shut.

Novak trundled the corpse through the darkness until the dolly hit the side of the sofa. He stood still and listened. The snores were rhythmic now. Julia Boyd was light-years away.

Using his thigh as a lever he got the heavy body onto the sofa. Theatrical arrangement wasn't important. He blinked his flash at the late Chalmers Boyd and wheeled the dolly out of the room. Closing the door he wiped his prints from the knob and hurried the dolly back to the service closet.

For a while he leaned weakly against the wall, breathing deeply until the dizziness left him. Then slowly he walked toward Paula's door.

6

"God," she breathed. "I thought you'd never get back. What'd you do with him?"

"You'll hear about it in time. The less you know the better. When the body's found there'll be more cops here than dogfaces on D-Day." He slumped into a chair. "You bring the bottle this time—with a couple of fresh aspirin on the half-shell."

She did as she was told. Novak washed down four aspirin with Scotch whisky. Cold out of the bottle it tasted like the edge of a knife.

Standing beside him, she stroked hair back from his forehead. Her hands were cool. Closing his eyes he felt her mouth brush his cheeks. "Kissing's nice," he murmured sleepily.

"Very nice. But what about your condition?"

"I've had worse nights. And I could use a shower."

After a while he got up, went into the bathroom, stripped and braced himself under a hot shower until the pain dulled. Then he toweled himself, pulled on his shorts and went into the sitting room.

The only light came from a table lamp by the far wall. He had to squint to see her, and when he did she was an indistinct swirl of white gauze on the sofa. "Hello,

Novak," her voice came throatily across the room. "Feel better?"

"Some. Room for two there?"

"Let's try."

He sat beside her and kissed the tip of her nose. Her hands moved around his body, kneaded the flesh behind his neck.

They were warm hands now. He put his arms around her and drew her close. She nibbled his lip and said, "You're built like a buffalo, Novak. Including the pelt."

"Only pansies and actors shave their chests."

She laughed lightly. "I suppose you're thinking I do this with all the boys."

"It would be a waste of talent."

Her hands framed his face. "You're a kick," she murmured. "Tough as elephant hide and laying your neck on the block for a girl you've known barely six hours."

"Seven."

"Ummmmm. What did you do before you got into the hotel business?"

"A lot of things. Too many. And very few things I liked."

"You've got a funny job."

"Well, you get to know a lot of drunks. And upper crust lushes."

He felt her face wrinkle. "I guess I hadn't better leave tomorrow, had I?"

"Stay around a few days. Act innocent."

"Be sensible. What about Ben?"

"He'll have to find a new girl."

"Uh-huh." Then her mouth covered his hotly. He felt her flimsy gown slide apart, the fullness of her breasts. Her eyelids fluttered shut.

The last thing he saw was the table lamp, an orange eye in the distant darkness.

"We could send out for something to drink."

He was tying his tie. "Too late. This is a scissorbill town. You can't buy a drink after midnight. Legitimately."

"The law worry you a lot?"

"Just worries me enough."

"What are you going to do about...Chalmers?"

"Give the police full cooperation. They don't pay me to solve murders. Not the Tilden chain."

"No ambition, Pete?"

Turning, he saw the glow of her cigarette from the sofa. "It's a disease I went through long ago."

"Along with a woman, maybe?"

"Along with a woman." He pulled on his coat, patted the holster into place.

"Married?"

"We were married," he said quietly. "She tired of it. She wanted bigger things—more than a mortgaged bungalow with time payments on the appliances."

He saw gray smoke drift into the arc of light near the bathroom door. Huskily she said, "I wish I'd known you then—before her."

"Hell, I haven't changed much. A little older and grayer, but they say the richer years come later."

"Not to a woman they don't. That's what I told myself. We're a couple of characters, you and I—and not out of fairy tales. Me, looking for a guy to keep me in furs and caviar, you—wrestling drunks and hopheads out of lobbies. Or is there more to life than that?"

"I wouldn't know." He straightened his lapels. "The job buys whisky and clean sheets. In today's world only a sap would complain." He crossed the room, bent down and kissed her forehead. "See you tomorrow, beautiful. Thanks for the tender care."

Her arms arched upward, her hands lowered his lips against hers. It was a long kiss. And a long time since he had known a kiss like that. Finally he parted her arms, patted the back of her hand and let himself out of the door.

Across the corridor only a closed door: Suite 515. Thirty-five bucks a day plus District Tax. Rate about to be lowered for single occupancy. He turned and made for the service elevator.

When the doors opened he saw the night watchman nodding in his chair. My alert security force, he thought, and eased around the corner and out to the street.

In the early dawn the trees were bony arms with fingers like ancient women. A newspaper truck whizzed around the corner, a heavy stack of newspapers bounced against the lamppost. Like a lazy black beetle a prowl car crawled down K Street. Lighting a cigarette, Novak coughed and turned up his coat lapels. The cold new morning was as gray as smoke. As he walked toward Seventeenth the streetlights flickered out. The night was over, a new day beginning.

A woman with a cloth bundle shuffled toward him,

kerchief around her head. Sagging brown cotton stockings, palms whitened from years of alkali soap. As she passed he heard tuneless humming. Something to ease the loneliness.

Getting into his car he thought: she could have had another gun. Maybe she shot him after all.

7

At eight o'clock a maid with a passkey opened the door
of Suite 515, took one startled look at the sofa and ran
shrieking down the hall. In the confusion that followed, no one thought to call Novak. He strolled into
his office at nine-thirty. By then the black bag boys had
photographed the body, dusted the room for prints
and trundled the remains of Chalmers Boyd away in a
mortuary basket. By a rear door, according to standard
procedure. The prints found on the doorknob were
those of the semi-hysterical maid who kept screaming
she was used to walking in on sleeping drunks, not
murdered corpses.

The man who brushed past Novak's secretary wore a
brown suit, not new, not old; a gray hat, stained around
the band, a maroon tie and a big gold and zircon ring
of some fraternal order. He was a short man with the
serious face of a hungry beagle. The frizzle of gray-
black beard on his face showed that he had gone on
duty sometime during the night. Novak had done business with him before. He was Detective Lieutenant
Morely, District Homicide.

As he eased into a chair across from Novak, he said,
"I get all the dirty ones. I oughta grab my retirement

and hire out on a job like this. Nice clean office, chic secretary, readable files and nothing to do but collect saddle boils."

"You wouldn't like it." Novak took a box of hotel cigars from a desk drawer, opened it. He pushed the box across the desk to Morely. "Too many straw bosses."

"Yeah," Morely grunted, selecting two cigars. He stowed one in his upper coat pocket, slicked cellophane from the other with a broad thumbnail, bit off the end and lighted up. He straightened his legs and eased back into the chair. A gust of blue smoke issued from his mouth.

Novak said, "How's the widow taking it?"

"The way a fat woman takes anything. Her story is she took some sleep syrup last night and turned in. Next thing she heard was the maid screaming. Boyd was supposed to have been at a convention banquet downstairs from eight-thirty on. But so far nobody remembers seeing him." He made a sour face. "Three hundred half-soused loan sharks scooping up filet mignon and French fries wouldn't notice a Cape Buffalo charging down the table. Much less a missing colleague." He stared down at his scuffed shoes. "We ought to be getting stuff on Boyd from Winnetka sometime today. The way the fat lady talked he pulled his share of weight around there." Squinting at Novak he muttered, "That guy Bikel's a weirdie. Another ten minutes and he'd have had me on a diet of stewed acorns and papaya seeds. Calls himself a doctor."

"A much-abused title," Novak said. "When I was a freshman I called a professor Professor. He got pretty mad—told me the only professors he knew about were musicians, acrobats and mountebanks. So I called him Doctor after that. Brickyard Charley Bates, the campus rock king."

Morely drew the cigar from his lips, patted a wrapper leaf into place and shrugged. "Know anything about Boyd I'm not likely to?"

"Well, the Boyds checked in three days ago bringing Bikel as a retainer. Then last evening the lady reported a quantity of jewels missing. Insured value ninety gees. I told her to report it to the Theft Squad."

Morely's eyebrows lifted. "Did she?"

"Not as far as I know. Her late husband hurried down here to explain the whole thing as a big mistake; wife subject to hysterical delusions. He credited Bikel with having had some success in treating her."

"What about the dazzlers?"

"Locked in his office safe in Winnetka."

Morely drew a frayed brown notebook from his coat, made a brief note and put it away. "We can check that when the safe's opened by the state tax people. Sounds interesting. Anything else?"

"Nothing relating to Boyd's death."

Morely shifted his weight, scratched his right ankle and stared at Novak. "Give, buddy," he snapped.

Novak sighed. "When I was leaving Mrs. Boyd last night I ran into a Chicago gambler—Ben Barada. The Tilden's conservative about floating dice games so I booted him out. Ben didn't like it. Not at all. In fact he later sent around a pair of punks to work me over. They jumped me in the alley and got the point across. I've got a scab on my scalp and my chest looks like a bad job of tattooing."

Morely grunted. "Making a complaint?"

Novak shook his head. "I'll settle with Barada—if we ever meet again."

Morely's mouth made a thoughtful sucking sound. "There wasn't any gun, Pat. That's what I don't like. Not even an ejected shell. Nothing to show Boyd was killed where he was found. Close to a contact wound, by the singed cloth and only internal bleeding. Heart penetration. The ME says he must have dropped like an elephant. Because of the warm room the ME can't fix death within three hours." He shook his head disgustedly. "Any time from eight last night until five this morning. That's what I got to work with." He stood up. "Oh, yeah. One of Boyd's business partners is a Congressman—Representative Barjansky. So I can expect federal pressure on this one." His fingers rotated the cigar between his lips. "Naturally I'd appreciate any help you can manage."

Novak stood up. "You know Tilden policy—complete cooperation with law enforcement authorities."

Morely's eyes regarded him humorously. "Except when we find a nest of hustlers operating in one of your fancy suites. Then cooperation's the last thing we get."

"We've got three hundred and forty rooms here. I can't shake down every one on the hour. Hell, this is a city within a city."

"Keep it clean," Morely murmured, and went out of the office.

Novak waited until the door closed and then he blotted his forehead with a handkerchief. Morely was an old-school cop, not one of the bright young crime-lab detectives. He hoped he had said enough to satisfy Morely. And if Morely stumbled onto Paula later he couldn't accuse Novak of not mentioning the Barada run-in.

Mary got up from her desk and brought over a typed letter. Novak signed it standing. "Seal the package with red wax," he told her. "Send the envelope registered, insured, return receipt requested. Just in case the blonde's left Cleveland by now."

Mary nodded. "A shame you don't get a reward, Pete."

"Well, I get the inner satisfaction of a job well done."

"There's always that." She went to the safe, took out the jewels he had recovered from Murky's room and carried the letter and the envelope to her desk. Novak went into the coffee shop and sat down at the counter. The waitress had a starched cap perched above her auburn hair, hazel eyes and a turned-up freckled nose. "Well, well," she said, polishing the counter in front of Novak. "God's gift to the weaker sex."

"Middle-aged members only," Novak bantered. "Coffee, Jerry. Hot and black as sin."

"And sweet as secret seduction?" She turned around, drew a cup and put it in front of him.

Novak grinned. "Young love. It's been years since I even thought of it. How's art school, kid?"

"Fashion design," she corrected. "Pretty good. One more term and Manhattan, here I come. And will I be glad—no more dirty plates and tarnished dimes."

Novak sipped the coffee. It was hot enough, but weak. He told her so. "Argue with the management," she said saucily. "Or take up Postum and mix your own."

"I might at that. Haven't been sleeping too well."

"Couldn't guess why," she said wickedly. "You and that young-old face of yours. That's something I'll miss on the Big Island."

Novak shook sugar into the cup and stirred lightly. "Sounds like pillowtalk, redhead."

"Not to me it doesn't. I'm holding out for a ring."

"The lonely crowd," Novak sighed. "Just pass me the check."

She made a mock-mad face. "Just try and get one." Then she flounced off to another customer.

A good kid, Jerry. Looks, spirit and maybe even talent. She might just make a go of it in New York. In one of those houses featuring fruity young men in pipestem velvet and skullfaced women with voices like stevedores. At least she was making her try. And on her own.

Jimmy Grant was patting his sleeve. "Pete, front office wants you. Right away."

"What's the beef?"

"The dead guy, I guess. Mr. Boyd—the one who got murdered last night."

Novak slid off the stool. "Murder, was it? Is Mr. Connery all nervous and upset-like?"

"They oughta diaper him today."

Novak chuckled, pushed through louvered walnut doors and crossed the lobby to the Assistant Manager's office.

Ralph Connery was in his late forties, a neat dresser with thin fingers and lips. Hairline deeply scalloped and a narrow bony nose that gave his voice a nasal quality. He was wearing a heather herringbone suit and a tab collar shirt and his eyes looked desperate.

"Where the hell have you been, Novak?"

"Out milking the pigeons."

Lips drew back showing brittle white teeth. "That's a wisecrack, I suppose. Well, we don't pay you for vaudeville chatter, as you've been told before."

Novak leaned forward slowly. "Hold down the aggressive impulses, Ralph," he said softly. "Where I've been is in my office listening to Detective Lieutenant Morely describe the morning's unpleasant discovery."

Connery's eyes shifted. "You weren't around," he complained. "I had to handle the police myself."

"Nobody notified me. And the police don't take much handling. They know their business. They get a pretty steady workout on DOA's."

"Even so," Connery muttered, "it was damned unpleasant. I understand you know Mrs. Boyd—the widow."

"Met her last night. Lost and found matter."

"Well, she wants you to come up. Now. And for God's sake, try to show a little sympathy. Where the Boyds come from they're important people."

"I'm deeply impressed. Shall I rent striped pants and a carnation before I make my call?"

Connery wet his lips. "Just go. And remember Mrs. Boyd may be difficult. Shock—you know."

"Yeah," Novak said pushing back at his chair. "I

know. Fortunately her medicine man's at hand. He'll be a world of help."

As Novak reached the elevator bank Jimmy sidled over to him. "Pete, remember that luscious number with the gray luggage who checked in last evening?"

"Thought about her all night."

"Me too. Well, she just drifted across the lobby and half the guys wheeled around and followed her out. Miss Paula Norton. Whatta dish."

Novak gave him a fake belly punch, tapped his chin with the other hand. "Too mature for you, sonny. Save your dough and shop for something your own age."

"But, Daddy, that's the one I want."

Elevator doors opened and Novak rode up to the fifth. It was getting to be the only floor in the hotel.

No uniformed policeman posted at the door. Not even a plainclothes man lurking down the corridor. A door like any other door. Novak ran his tongue over his teeth and pressed the bell.

The man who opened the door was Dr. Edward Bikel. He stared gravely at Novak and intoned, "A dreadful tragedy, sir. Mrs. Boyd is containing herself with great forebearance. She has displayed a truly marvelous spirit. I entreat you not to upset her."

Novak gave him a glassy smile. "I'm the picker-upper, Doc. They keep me around mainly for morale purposes. Is the widow under sedation?"

A nerve started to work in Bikel's cheek. His eyes flickered. "As a matter of fact, I administered something mild and soothing. No laboratory product, Mr. Novak. Just a simple, natural remedy."

Novak's voice became hard as he said, "I'd hold it to that, Doc. The Narco Squad would love to get their hands on an out-of-towner passing out prescription drugs." He moved past Bikel and crossed the sitting room. Where Boyd had lain the pillows were plumped out. Everything was as sterile and impersonal as a stage-setting.

He knocked on the half-open bedroom door and in a moment Julia Boyd's voice told him to enter.

She was propped up in one of the twin beds, wearing a lacy, salmon-colored bed jacket that did nothing for her muddy complexion. A ravaged tray on the other bed gave every indication that Julia Boyd had break-fasted heartily.

One puffy hand lifted and signaled him closer. Novak drew a chair to the side of the bed and murmured, "You have my sympathy, Mrs. Boyd."

Harshly she said, "Chalmers Boyd was a skunk, Mr. Novak. After our marriage I realized he had married me for my money. Back in Winnetka I'll have to put on a show of grief, but here—among strangers—I refuse to be hyprocritical. Do you have a cigarette?"

Novak gave her one, lighted it and closed the bed-room door.

Behind the veil of smoke her eyes narrowed. "What's that for?"

"It's likely the doc wouldn't approve. Tobacco's a wicked weed."

Her throat gave forth a deep chortle. "S'what he keeps telling me. He's right, of course, but I haven't many pleasures left."

Novak resumed his seat and said nothing.

Julia Boyd blew a jet of smoke toward the ceiling. After a while she said, "My late husband visited you last night."

"True."

"I want to know the subject of the discussion."

"I'd guess you know it already."

Her head moved to one side. "Chalmers went to tell you I had delusions; that the jewelry I said was missing wasn't missing at all. Am I right?"

Novak nodded.

"Did he mention where it was?"

"He said it was in his office safe."

She laughed unpleasantly. "A damn lie, Mr. Novak. Chalmers didn't have it, I didn't have it either. Not for a long time."

"You lied to me, Mrs. Boyd?"

"Yes, I lied to you. For practical reasons. So the slut he gave my jewelry to would never be able to enjoy it. So that she'd be forced to return it. And for a price considerably under what she was asking."

"This is all getting pretty involved, Mrs. Boyd. Frankly, I don't know why you're confiding these unpleasant facts to me."

She sat up and rolled her bulk toward him. "I'll tell you why, Novak. Because there's a job I want done and I think you can do it for me. You look hard and you talk tough and that's the kind of a man I need." She was leaning on one elbow staring at him, her little eyes shiny as beetle backs. "Well, what about it?"

"I haven't heard what you have in mind, Mrs. Boyd."

"Call me Julia. What I have in mind is recovering the jewelry Chalmers gave to that little bitch he was keeping. How you get it back, I don't care. The point is I want it. And it's worth a thousand dollars to you."

Novak fanned himself lightly. "A lot of money, Mrs. Boyd—Julia. I'm Pete, by the way. Plus travel expenses to Winnetka?"

She snorted. "No traveling involved. All you have to do is cross the hall and twist my jewelry out of the woman in that room. Her name is Paula Barada. What she's registered as I haven't the faintest idea. Well?"

"She was your husband's mistress?"

"Unless the detective I hired reported nothing but lies."

"Do you think she was responsible in any way for your husband's death?"

"I certainly do!" she screeched. "I told that police lieutenant all about her."

Novak stood up. "The wise thing to do. For now I'd leave it with the police. Slander can cost a pile of money."

"Well," she snapped, "are you taking the job?"

Novak pursed his lips. "Cases of this sort can run into surprising difficulties. For now I'll reconnoiter the ground—see what the lady looks like first. A little caution could pay off."

"Don't be too damn cautious," she bristled. "For my thousand dollars I expect action."

The door opened and Bikel slid in. "Julia, you must remain calm. Please. We mustn't have one of your spells now."

82 E. HOWARD HUNT

Staring at him levelly she spat. "Drop dead, Eddie."

Bikel choked, colored and disappeared.

Julia Boyd watched the retreat with evident plea-
sure. "That creep," she snarled, "may well be my next
husband."

Novak blinked. "He won't last."

"And why not?"

"You'll eat him alive and stuff the skin for your bedroom."

Julia Boyd cackled hoarsely. "I like you, Novak—
Pete, is it? You say what you think. Yes. A man spending
my money owes me certain obligations. Chalmers forgot his. You may go now. But I expect to hear from you.
Understand?"

"You won't care if I break a couple of her arms?"

She chortled greedily. "I'd love it. Now get busy."

Novak went out of the bedroom and saw Bikel
slumped in a chair staring out of the window. "Brace
up, Doc," he said cheerfully. "Everyone has days like
this. A little pink pepsin compound ought to calm her
down."

Bikel shot him a venomous glance. Novak opened
the door and went out.

8

As he walked down the corridor he shook out a cigarette, moistened dry lips and lighted it. So Julia Boyd had known about Paula and her hubby. That was a small item Morely had neglected to pass along. Already Paula was under a degree of suspicion.

Paula thought she had the jewelry safely hidden, then found out it was missing. Maybe Boyd had waited until Paula went out, opened her door somehow and searched for the jewelry. Maybe he had found it, then later got himself killed. For what? For the jewels? Or maybe the murder of Boyd and the theft of the jewels were two unrelated happenings. Barada had been in a wild mood last night. He had plenty of reason to resent Boyd. Suppose he came back for another chat with Paula and found Boyd there, with or without Paula. Maybe Barada had pulled a gun and shaken down Boyd for the ninety grand payoff money, drilled him and waltzed away with the jewels to boot.

So far he had been accepting Paula's version as close to the truth. Of what other things she might be guilty he didn't care. He had believed her last night, believed her enough to move the corpse from its compromising location. But Julia Boyd had pushed her into a hot skillet anyway. Before Morely did anything he would take a hard look at the evidence, at where the threads wound. Then, if he were convinced, he would move in ruthlessly.

"What if she killed him?" he said half-aloud, and thought, how far would you go to save her?

Not a centimeter, a voice said coldly. Then another voice: You'd want to find out why she did it. Then make up your mind.

"Yeah," he said to the empty hall. "That's what you'd do."

Back in his office Novak phoned the Credit Central and asked for traces on Bikel. Lighting a cigarette he stared through the Venetian blinds at the sunny street. Whir of traffic, click of heels, chatter of voices. The outside world.

A grand from Julia Boyd to get back jewelry from Paula Norton who no longer had it. Who, then? The murderer, probably, but no long odds on that, either. Or had Paula staged a little act for his benefit? In the normal course of events Boyd would have gone to her room with the payoff money and walked out with the jewelry. Suppose he had gone there and tried to strong-arm the jewels from Paula. Novak could see her shooting Boyd, hiding the gun and the jewels and phoning him. Hell, he should have searched Boyd's body when he had the chance. For jewels or money or both. Now it was too late.

He dialed Paula's room, heard the phone buzz a dozen times and hung up.

Mary carried over some morning registrations that had been credit-checked. Novak initialed them and dropped them in his OUT box. A new day at the Tilden. New faces, new names. Traveling men, lobbyists, grifters, old folks seeing the Nation's Capital. A city of overnight guests. The largest floating population in the country. A city of parks and highways and museums. With marble and granite buildings that looked as hospitable as a county jail.

The phone rang. Mary answered and buzzed Novak.

The caller was Lieutenant Morely. "Thought you'd like to know," he said in a voice frayed with fatigue. "We scooped a sample of the widow's sleepy tonic. Whattaya know—under the cherry flavor it's loaded with mescaline. No wonder fatty gets hallucinations. I guess we wouldn't have to look far to find the source of supply."

"No," Novak said. "About as far as the luggage of a certain nature doctor. You figure she was asleep last night when the shooting took place?"

"Well, the syrup's got a high enough percentage to make her crazy as a dancing bear. Of course, we don't know when Boyd caught his bullet or when Mrs. Boyd went to bed. Or whether she really took that syrup last night. Or—if she did, how much?"

Novak said, "Bikel's from near the Mex border where the Indians brew mescaline from peyote buttons. For the Rain Dance or whatever the hell they celebrate these days. Picking him up?"

"Not just yet. Any sign of either one checking out, let me know. I'm going home to grab me some shut-eye but the desk can reach me."

"Will do," Novak said. "Any other leads?"

"Yeah, that hood Barada's wife is a guest at the Tilden. A looker. Signed in as Miss Norton."

Novak's fingers tightened around the receiver. "You don't say."

Morely yawned. "There was something steamy between her and the dear departed. With Barada around, looks like it could have been the badger game. Work hard, pal."

The phone went dead.

Novak replaced the receiver and wiped his palms on his thighs. Morely had worked fast. He had Bikel where he could squeeze him if the need arose. Even homebrew mescaline was on the list of controlled narcotics.

He thought about visiting Paula's room and shaking it down. But if she had a second gun it was gone by now. The same with any jewelry. Too late for that now. Hours too late.

As he passed Mary's desk he said, "If Connery wants me I'm following up a request by Mrs. Boyd. Be back in an hour."

Walking across the lobby he signaled Jimmy Grant and said, "If you see Miss Norton come back, make a note of the time and leave it on my desk."

"Sure, Pete." His face was mystified. "Worried about a skip?"

"That would be the least of my worries," he muttered, and went out to the street.

The air was as crisp and cool as mountain mint. Novak gulped it down, tossed away his cigarette and bought a morning paper. The Boyd death was a page 18 paragraph. No details were given and the Tilden was described only as a downtown hotel. He folded the newspaper and dropped it in the corner trash basket. Another block and the cement and glass brick front of Robinson's Veterinary Hospital. The reception girl went through an inner door and Novak could hear the yapping of assorted pets. The door closed. After a while Doc Robinson came out wearing a white hospital gown.

Novak said, "I sent you a client last night, Doc. A little toy Skye terrier."

Robinson pulled off rubber gloves, wiped his rimless glasses and consulted a register. "Named Toby," he said.

"His mistress got worried about him last night and came down here. Would you have a record of the time?"

"We admitted an Angora kitten and a Dalmatian last night but no visitors came by."

"You were here how long?"

The vet frowned. "Oh, maybe eleven-thirty."

"And Miss Norton—the Skye's owner—didn't stop by?"

"Not according to my records. She didn't mention it when she came here a little while ago, either."

"Oh?"

"She collected her pup and took him out for a stroll. Hasn't returned yet."

"Any ideas where she might have gone?"

"I suggested Farragut Park."

"Thanks, Doc."

"No trouble, Pete."

The door opened and a woman entered, tugging at a boxer on a heavy chain. "Well, well," the vet said in a cheery professional voice, "What seems to be the trouble today, Mrs. Tannenbaum?"

Novak eased himself out of the closing door. Setting his teeth he strode toward Farragut Square.

She was there, all right, hatless and in her mink coat, sitting on a park bench. The Skye was chasing pigeons nearby. Her head was tilted back and her eyes were closed. As Novak sat down beside her the Skye yapped protectively. He said, "Got a light, lady?"

"Dust, buster," she said coldly, then opened her eyes. "You!" she said with a little gasp. "One thing about this town—half the men are on the make."

"Any town." Novak lighted a cigarette and gave it to her.

"Is this a chance encounter or were you looking for me?"

"A little of each. You said you went out to the vet's last night."

"I did."

"Doc Robinson says you didn't."

Her eyes narrowed. "I said I went out to see Toby. I didn't say I'd seen him. When I got to the hospital there was an awful fuss going on. An animal yapping and the owners carrying on. So I didn't go in. I just walked around for a while and went back to my room. Anything else?"

"A small thing: Boyd's widow called me in a while back. Seems she'd had detectives following the late Chalmers for quite a while. Long enough to learn about your connection with the dear departed."

She sat forward, breath hissing inward between set teeth. "What else did she know?"

"She knew you had her jewelry and that her husband was trying to get it back. She knows you're here." He crossed his legs and leaned back, blinking from the sun. "And she's offered me a thousand dollars to get the gems back from you. Even if I have to break your pretty arms."

Her face was frozen. "That's a lot of money in your league, Novak."

"Some weeks I don't see the half of it, gray-eyes. Not only that, she's told the police about you and hubby and suggested strongly that you were responsible for his death."

The cigarette dropped from her fingers. The Skye bounced over, but she told him to go away. Moistening her lips she said huskily, "Pete, I've got to get out of here."

He shook his head slowly. "Absolutely the worst idea I've heard today. If you didn't shoot him you're in no danger."

"You think I did?"

"It's at least a possibility. I can visualize Boyd going to your room and jumping you for the jewels. I can see you grabbing a gun and shooting him to protect yourself. Then calling Sunny Jim to cart off the corpse."

"And paying you off with my smooth white body," she said bitterly. "What a lovely mind you have, Mr. Novak. I suppose keyhole peeping breeds thoughts like that."

"Possibly," he said, "but we aren't discussing me at the moment. We're talking about a murder and some missing jewelry. We both know where the corpse is. What I don't know is where the jewelry is."

"And you think I do," she said dully. The Skye jumped onto her lap and she held it between folded arms.

"Let's say I'm wondering if you've been entirely frank with me. At the moment the jewels are sort of a key item. If you've got them, get rid of them in a way that won't lead back to you. If you haven't, then you've no reason to worry."

One hand ran back through her ash-blonde hair. She laughed thinly. "God, what a fool I was. I let myself think you were…" Her voice trailed away. "The hell with that. Well, I don't have the jewels and I didn't kill Chalmers—despite any ideas you may have to the contrary. Now would you mind leaving me alone with my thoughts, Novak? I'll try to dryclean them here in the sun and fresh air."

He got up from the bench. The Skye twitched its tail and stared up at him balefully. Novak said, "Where's Big Ben Barada hanging out?"

Her lips clamped together and she shook her head. He thought he could see tiny, moist diamonds in her lashes.

"Answer the man," he said roughly. "Don't be a sucker all your life. Your ex-husband's been playing a part in this from the beginning. From just the little you've told me, he was desperate for money. To him money or jewels would have equal value. That's enough for motive. I can see him letting himself into your empty room and waiting for Boyd to show, killing him and lifting the payoff roll and the jewelry as well. He'd lived with you long enough to know where you'd be likely to hide something valuable. I want to know if he's left town. If so the police would be glad to have the information. There are a few questions he could answer."

Her head lifted and she stared dumbly at him, eyes foggy with tears.

Novak said, "Why make me do it the hard way? If he's still here he'll be calling you. I can have the hotel switchboard trace all calls to your room." He shrugged. "All right, go on taking his lumps. You're in a tough spot, beautiful. The cops aren't in any mood to write off this one."

Suddenly her chin dropped, her shoulders shook. The terrier licked her cheek. After a while she dabbed her eyes and said unevenly, "He's in a motel on the road to Alexandria. The Vernon."

"Room number?"

"Thirty-seven."

"That's better," Novak said. "And let's not make any calls before I get there. I'd hate to have to shoot my way in."

"But you would," she said tightly.

"After what his punks fed me last night I'd welcome the chance. Meanwhile, give doggie a nice long airing and think wholesome thoughts."

Bitterly she said, "You really put your heart into your work. A thousand dollars is cheap for what you're willing to do. From now on I'll bolt my door at night."

Turning, he walked away from her. As he crossed toward the Army and Navy Club he glanced back and saw her staring vacantly at the sidewalk. He hung a cigarette in his mouth, but it did nothing for the bitter taste, and he flicked it away savagely.

His mouth took on a crooked set, he squared his shoulders and muttered, "You're hell with the ladies, killer. Ought to finish off the morning slapping around a white-haired old mom for kicks."

He walked two blocks rapidly and turned into a bar with flaked English script on the windows: *The Hunters' Lodge*. The inside was dark and musty with a permanent odor of stale peanuts and potato chips. "Irish," he snapped at the bartender.

"Hold on, buddy, there's plenty of time. Water or soda?"

"Ice, pal. I skate better than I swim."

At the far end, a waiter mopping down the floor, chairs upended on tables. A couple arguing in a side booth. Married probably. You don't develop subjects for sustained argument until you've been married awhile.

The bartender shoved an Old Fashioned glass at him, covered chipped ice from a metal jigger. Novak stirred it with one finger, lifted it and tossed it off. "Encore," he said and gripped the round bar edge with his hands.

As the bartender sloshed more whisky over the ice he said, "Whassa matter? Trouble with the girlfriend?"

Novak stared at him. "You could say that and have a fifty-percent chance of being right. Anyone could."

"Yeah, the other being money. That's what it all boils down to here at the bar: dames or dough. I see plenty of it. The things I hear from this side would make a novel a day. Trouble is I don't know any writers. You know one, send him around, I'll collaborate cheap."

"Facts aren't good enough," Novak said and downed the drink. "The writing guys always have to gaudy them up." He pulled out five dollars and waited for change. The bartender rang up two whiskies and slapped the change on the counter. "Drop by any time," he said. "Glad to have the business."

Novak pushed out to the sidewalk, blinked at the sunlight and covered the last two blocks to his garage. He unlocked the door, backed out the Pontiac and turned south for the Fourteenth Street Bridge.

On the road to Alexandria.

9

The Vernon Motor Hotel was one of twenty-odd between Washington and Alexandria, set back off the highway on a lush rise of emerald grass. Between the transplanted elms a shiny hardtop drive wound toward the center Georgian portico. On either side of the lobby building brick wings curved back, each unit served by its own driveway and porte-cochere. It looked clean, tidy and expensive as a Caribbean cruise. Novak parked on the main drive and cut across the lawn.

There was no car beside Number 37. That could mean something or nothing. As he walked he loosened his revolver in its holster and eyed the doorway ahead. A white-jacketed waiter was pedaling a shiny red bicycle along the sidewalk, balancing a covered tray on his padded head. Novak watched him park the bike, dismount and ring a doorbell.

When the waiter had disappeared inside, Novak stepped up to the door numbered 37 and pressed the button. Then he stepped to one side.

From a shade elm a robin swooped toward the grass, lighted and began stalking over the close-cropped greenery, cocking its head from side to side. From inside Number 37 no sound of moving feet, no shouted query. Novak rang again, wondering if Barada was driving his own car these days.

Still no answer.

Looking around, Novak waited until the waiter was pedaling back toward the kitchen and then he turned the doorknob. The door was locked. Glacing down he saw the lock was a cheap model with a keyhole in the pushbutton on the knob. He felt for his folder of spring-steel picks, selected one and went to work. Down the line a door opened and a man appeared lugging a heavy suitcase. His wife followed with an overnight bag and half a page of advice. Novak palmed the pick and stared at the white-painted door numbers. After a while he heard an engine start and when he glanced around, a blue Dodge with Arkansas plates was pulling away. Novak stepped close to the door and inserted the pick again. Finally the button popped out and the knob turned.

Novak went quickly inside and locked the door handle.

It was a two-room unit, small sitting room, bedroom and shower-bath. Novak clicked on a table lamp and looked around.

There were two suitcases, one open across the seat of a chair. It held some silk shirts, a couple of ties, a pair of alligator shoes with pointed toes, toilet gear and a bottle of rye. The writing table held an almost empty bottle of the same brand, two bottles that had once held ginger ale, a bucket of melted ice and three dirty glasses. He looked at the ashtrays. None of the butts had rouge on them.

The bed had been slept in. The corner held a tumble of dirty laundry. One of the shirts was blue silk, the one Barada had worn last night. In the bureau drawers, nothing but half a dozen monogrammed handkerchiefs.

Novak went back to the sitting room and listened. Then he knelt down and unstrapped the other suitcase. The catch was locked so he opened it with a small pick and unfolded the suitcase on the carpet.

More shirts and ties. Two sharkskin suits. A dozen packs of cards. A leather dice holder and eight ivory dice. A green box of cartridges, some of them missing. Caliber 7.65 mm. That meant Barada was wearing a gun that fired a slug about the size of the one that killed Chalmers Boyd.

Standing up Novak massaged his knees and broke the seal on the bottle of rye. He rinsed a little around his mouth, swallowed and made a sour face. Far from the best available. Recapping the bottle he dropped it back into the open suitcase. Then he turned off the table lamp, fitted himself into an armchair and waited in the darkness.

A car accelerated down the drive, tires squealing as it braked in the distance. Check-out probably. Then silence for a long time.

As he waited his ears grew sensitive. He could hear the whir of a vacuum somewhere in the same wing, goosey laughter from a couple next door, the splash of water in a swimming pool behind the wing.

Sun warming the roof made the joints expand and creak. Now that his eyes were accustomed to darkness, he could make out the furniture from where he sat. Another car idling along the drive. It seemed to slow in front of Number 37, then moved on and Novak let his breathing relax.

His body still pained him, but it was a dull pain today and the liquor was helping. His hands curled over the wooden ends of the chair arms and he flexed his muscles. The door would open any minute, bringing Big Ben Barada.

Then outside sounds seemed to fade away and he could hear only the uneasy creak of the timbers above.

The telephone rasped harshly.

The sound jerked him out of the chair. When he realized what it was he cursed softly and walked toward it. The sound came again, commanding and urgent. He hesitated, then picked up the receiver. Muffling it with his fingers he snapped, "Yeah?"

The voice was a distant disembodied whisper. It breathed, "We'll have to make it later. No earlier than nine o'clock."

"Why?"

"I'm being watched. I can't..." the voice dropped and grew suddenly urgent. "Got to hang up. I'll call later." The receiver clicked down.

Novak stared at the receiver in his hand, lowered it and went back to his chair. The call had been meant for Ben Barada. The voice could have been anyone's. No chance of tracing it.

His eyelids were heavy. He stretched out his feet and yawned. The liquor was making him sleepy. In the warm silent darkness he felt himself drifting away. Closing his eyes he slept.

He woke with a jerk, grabbing at his holster, then heard the car backfire again. A sports car with a noisy muffler. The engine caught, held, and the car *throomed* away. Blinking, he shook himself and stood up. His wristwatch showed 12:20. No telling when Barada might come back. Novak crossed to the door, pressed his ear to the panel and listened. No outside sounds. Opening the door a crack he peered out and then he eased through the doorway and began striding across the grass. A waiter pedaled past on a bicycle. A new station wagon pulled up in front of Number 35 and a bellhop helped the young couple unload. No one paid any attention to Novak. He got behind the wheel of his car, started the engine and drove back into Washington.

Mary was still out for lunch but she had left a typed message. Credit Central had called back with some information on Dr. Edward Bikel. He had done time in the forties for check altering, beat a federal rap for selling a phony cancer cure, and was last known to be in Chicago operating a health food store. His credit rating was zero. None of it was any surprise to Novak. He folded the sheet into his billfold and idled into the coffee shop. The redhead had gone off duty and the waitress who brought his Salisbury steak had a beak like a crow's and a face with more lines than a contour map. Novak sipped a pint of homogenized milk, drank a cup of coffee and signed the check. As he walked across the lobby Jimmy Grant drifted over. "She just got back, Pete. About five minutes ago. Anything else?"

Novak shook his head. "That's all for now, kid. Go hustle some shiny quarters." He went over to the elevators and rode one to the fifth floor. Stopping at Paula Norton's door he pushed the bell button.

After a while he heard her muffled voice. "Who is it?"

"Novak."

"Go away."

"A couple of words, beautiful."

The door opened the length of the snub chain. She was wearing a dressing gown and her feet were bare. "What is it?"

"All the way," he said. "I'm not going to beat you up. I'm not your ex-husband."

She shivered and the chain rattled free. Stepping back she let Novak enter. When the door was shut he said, "Ben wasn't there. I waited for him but no show. Only a phone call." He shrugged. "So much for that. I'm going to talk to fatty now, tell her I braced you for the jewelry but got nothing. That should hold her for now."

"Such faith in me," she sneered. "Sure it won't bend your professional ethics?"

His hands caught her wrists and held them until she stopped struggling. As he drew her to him he muttered, "After what I did for you last night my ethics show more curves than a pretzel. Remember that, beautiful." He pressed her lips against his and felt her body quiver and go slack. When he opened his eyes he saw that hers were glistening.

Huskily she said, "I had no right to say what I did. I guess I'm half-crazy with worry. Ben, the jewelry, the old lady…What I ought to do is get stone drunk."

"I've heard worse ideas."

"Can't I change to another room? Every time I go into the bedroom I think of Chalmers lying there. And the widow across the hall. Good Lord, I've never been in a spot like this."

"Since the police are mildly interested in you they might get even more interested if you changed your room. Waiting's tough but none of this would have happened if you hadn't started to exploit that streak of larceny in your beautiful body. At that you're getting off easy. If staying in your room is bad, think what it would be like down at Police Headquarters trying to explain away a dead lover in your bedroom. And I haven't even twisted your arms, the way I'll tell it to Mrs. Boyd. So, between highballs, count your blessings."

"I will," she said throatily. "I'll do everything you say."

Opening the door, he backed into the hallway.

Crossing to Suite 515, he rang the bell and waited.

Instead of Bikel, Julia Boyd opened the door. Her face registered surprise. "Oh, I thought it would be the police."

As he closed the door he said, "More questions?"

"Not that." She shrugged. "They aren't ready to release Chalmer's body for burial. I thought once an autopsy was over, the next of kin could claim the body."

"Not always. Guess that postpones your departure plans."

She patted the side of her hair with one pudgy hand. "I'm not leaving without my jewelry, Mr. Novak. Oh, no!" Turning she walked further into the room. Her stout legs were clad in bulging slacks. There were fluffy slippers on her bare feet. A heavy cotton brassiere showed through the lacy white blouse. "Well," she demanded, "did you get it from her?"

Novak shook out a cigarette and lighted it. "Not yet," he said slowly. "She was out all morning, just got back a little while ago. I moved in on her then." He smiled wolfishly. "A hard baby," he purred. "Took plenty of punishment."

Julia Boyd's face broke into a lustful smile. "You really beat her up, huh?"

"She's huddled up on the sofa sobbing like a baby." He blew smoke at the chandelier. "Look, Mrs. Boyd—Julia, I mean—I don't think she has the stuff. Either that or she's the toughest pigeon I ever pummeled."

"Nonsense. You can't handle her kind with velvet gloves. She's tough, all right—tough enough to kill my husband. Now go back there and get my jewelry."

Novak let himself down on the sofa and stared up at her. "Her ex-husband is in town—Ben Barada. That mean anything to you?"

"It means you'll have to work fast."

He shook his head slowly. "Barada's a factor we ought to consider. He's not long out of Joliet, and broke, the way she tells it. I figure he followed her here, latched onto the jewelry and blew town. Maybe he killed your husband in the process."

Her eyes were slits in an unbaked pie. "You gone soft on her?" she hissed.

"No, ma'am. I'm trying to find a logical answer— and your jewelry. Shoving her around didn't get us anywhere. Maybe there's another way." He let his voice trail off doubtfully.

"What?"

"Tell the police about Barada, let them haul him in and squeeze out what they can."

Her face seemed in deep thought. Finally she said, "No. I don't want that."

"Don't you want your husband's murderer caught?"

"I mainly want my jewelry back before she has a chance to cash it in and hire defense attorneys with my money."

Novak leaned back and gazed up at the cool green ceiling. "I don't think they'll arrest her," he said thoughtfully. "The body was found here and there's nothing to suggest she was ever in here, and logic's against your husband inviting her in. Alive he was a heavy man; dead he would be even heavier. Think a jury would believe a girl as slight as Paula could wrestle his dead weight through two doors and onto this sofa?"

Her face was the color of a ripe grape. "You fool," she wheezed, "I tell you that woman killed my husband. I insist you search her rooms and baggage. The evidence is there. It must be. That's not much to do for a thousand dollars."

Novak stood up. "Suppose I told you I'd searched her room and her bags—and found nothing."

Julia Boyd swore. "She's bought you off, that's what's happened. Damn, who can a helpless widow turn to?"

"Ed Bikel," Novak said. "He's about the size and build for a prowl job. And he can probably pick a lock as good as the next follow. Sorry we didn't make out as a team, Mrs. Boyd, but all this has been pretty far out of my usual line. You're a sturdy figure of a woman. Why not charge over there and take up where I left off?"

"You're walking out on me?"

"Guess so." He moved toward the doorway. "Oh, one thing, Mrs. Boyd. If you didn't know it before, that pink mixture Bikel doses you with is loaded with mescaline. Nightmare juice. No wonder you've been getting hallucinations. That's what the stuff's for."

"Mesca…mesca—*what?*" she stuttered, face paling.

"Mescaline. Where the Doc comes from, the Indians make a brew of buds from a special cactus plant. That's how they do those crazy stunts with snakes and hot coals. Their medicine men take it for visions. It stops time, turns the world green, purple and gold. Dangerous stuff, Mrs. Boyd—in non-professional hands. Now might be the time to change to something milder."

One hand clawed a roll of fat around her throat.

"The Doc's hanging by a thread. The law around here is all federal, and even possession is a crime. You might mention that to him the next time he ambles up with a teaspoon."

Opening the door he went out.

His hands felt clammy but his face wore a smile. As he walked along the corridor he saw Bikel's door jerk open. Novak stopped, half-turned and fussed with his cigarette. The sound of angry voices reached along the corridor. A door slammed and Novak turned.

Someone was running toward the elevators.

Novak jogged, slowed and saw a woman pressing the DOWN button. As he strolled quietly toward her he heard a sound of sniffling, saw her fumble a handkerchief from her purse, dry her eyes and blow her nose. She was breathing in quick gasps. A little birdlike woman in an old blue rayon dress, a black straw hat with a half-veil and scuffed black walking shoes. The elevator door opened and they entered together. Her shoulders moved jerkily and she kept her face covered with the handkerchief. Once he thought he heard a stifled moan, but it could have been only a strain on the elevator cable.

When the doors slid apart she straightened and buried the handkerchief in her purse. Her thin lips were almost colorless but her cheeks were flushed. Gray streaks threaded her hair. The skin of her hands was roughened, the knuckles large. A woman who was no stranger to hard labor. As she left the elevator Novak followed her through the lobby and out to the street. She hesitated for a moment, then turned and walked up Seventeenth Street.

Novak expected her to hail a taxi or head for a streetcar stop but she crossed the intersection with quick, determined steps and Novak followed. The light held him and when he could cross she was nearly a block away. At Rhode Island she turned left and scurried around to the side door of a brownstone

Gothic church. When Novak reached the door he saw a legend above it in old English script: *Chapel. Enter and Meditate. Join the Fellowship of Prayer.*

He felt sorry for the little woman. There had been strong, bitter words between her and Bikel and now she was in the chapel seeking consolation and strength. As he thought about her kneeling in the dimness, he felt a surge of dislike toward Bikel. That smug fraud. What right did he have to bring unhappiness to anyone? Novak weighed going in and talking to her, but being approached by a stranger might upset her even more.

Moodily he walked back to the Tilden.

10

The Cuban challenger sported a cut right eye and a
bloody ear. The Negro danced around him, grinning
and worrying his face. The Cuban's legs got wobbly.
He threw a wild left at the Negro, missed and staggered against the ropes. As he bounced off, the Champ
primed him with a short right to the chin. A stiff left
doubled the Cuban and a right cross tumbled him. He
rolled over, got one elbow on the canvas and conked
out. The referee jumped into the ring and grabbed the
Negro's arm. The Champ was still Champ. On a TKO.
Novak got out of his chair, turned off the TV and
lighted a table lamp. The fights were getting worse
every year. What with the tax bite, the incentive was
dropping away. The Champ made most of his dough
from Harlem and Detroit real estate, not fighting. And
a chain of soft drink stands. Not that you ever found
the Champ in one. He was off sipping tall cool ones in
the better cabarets and sobering up in Turkish baths.
But even on skis the Champ could have atomized the
Cuban.

Novak built himself a short drink in the kitchenette
and carried it back to his living room. Not even eleven
yet; the waltz had lasted only five rounds of the sched-
uled fifteen.

Novak sipped his drink and yawned.

The phone rang jarringly. Novak got up and answered. The voice said, "Morely. You doing anything special?"

"Fighting off boredom."

"Good. I'm not too far away. I'll drop by." The line clicked off. Novak went into his kitchenette, set a globe of coffee water on the electric range. He measured coffee carefully into a filter cone and assembled the apparatus. By the time he had finished, the door buzzer was sounding. He pressed the lock-release button for the alley door and Morely's footsteps trudged upward.

He was clean-shaven and his suit had been pressed within the month. He dropped his hat on a chair and rubbed his hands together. "Not a bad set-up you got here."

"It's cheap, anyway. Coffee's making."

"Let's lace it with a little something. Got an hour to kill the breath before I check in."

"That makes this an unofficial visit."

He shrugged. "You weren't busy. I figured we could slide our cards together and take a cold reading. Call it official or unofficial. Mox nix."

Novak went back to the kitchenette and brought back the coffee-maker and an asbestos pad. As the coffee was filtering, he got out cups and saucers and the sugar bowl. While Morely poured, Novak carried over a bottle of California brandy. Morely ignored the sugar and topped his cup with brandy. Then he leaned back in his chair, tasted and sighed. "Night duty. Three more weeks on night shift before I get to see my kids again. Around the flat I'm just a legend—the beardy guy snoring in the corner bedroom." He drank more of his coffee. "How far you figure the Senators will get this season?"

"About like last. Unless they buy a couple of hitters."

"Yeah. I hear they may get Frank Howard or Billy O'Dell on a trade."

"For what—the rest of the club?"

Morely chuckled and put his coffee down on the table. "Now we got the League's problems solved, let's look over the messy little lash-up down at your mattress store. First off, you were seen chatting with Barada's dame in the park this morning. What about it?"

"She was out walking her dog. I noticed her there."

Morely nodded slowly. "You seen Barada lately?"

"No."

"What about Mrs. Boyd?"

"She complains you guys won't release the corpse so she can bury and forget him."

"That's how we're keeping her in town. Her and the witch doctor. Maybe they'll get nervous enough to tell us something we'd like to hear."

Novak shook his head. "Julia's in no hurry. Any nerves she has are well padded with lard. While you guys sweat, all she has to do is hibernate."

"You maybe got something there. Oh, yeah, the slug we fished out of her husband told us damn little. Small caliber gun, but we got that mostly from the wound. Not much left of the slug after piercing the rib cage and spattering into the vertebra where we found it.

No riflings and too badly fragmented to identify by weight. The lab boys feel real bad but they look at things differently from me. Whoever gunned Boyd had a reason: avarice, fright, revenge. Like that. All the old ones. To find the killer all I have to do is figure the motive and match it to the right guy. I don't need no head-shrinkers or test-tube wizards to get the answers." He sipped his brandy-coffee. "Start throwing technical evidence at a jury and you got yourself a mountain of trouble. It's what defense shysters love to pick the most. For every expert the State gets on the stand, the defense can hire two more to give a conflicting story." He made a noisy sound with his lips. "What convinces juries is the old-fashioned combination clinching motive, opportunity and method. And that don't just materialize from a hypo of truth serum."

Novak got up and opened the window. When he went back to his chair Morely was squinting at the ceiling. "Wonder if you noticed something about the Boyd killing that jumped up and shouted at me."

"Afraid I haven't had your years of experience, Lieutenant."

Morely smiled indulgently. "When a gun goes off it makes a loud noise—even a small-bore pistol. Think anyone can convince me Boyd was shot in the sitting room and his drowsy missus never heard it?" He made a sour face. "Someone's lying. Either that or Boyd was shot elsewhere and taken back to his own place. If that's what happened it took not only strength but nerve. And I figure Boyd wasn't moved overly far." He shifted in his chair and stared at Novak. "The Barada dame's holed up across the hall and the Doc's down the way. I doubt the little lady coulda lugged him but the Doc might have. Or Barada himself."

Novak's face had grown cold. He flexed his fingers and stared at them. White scars showed where skates had slashed them years ago. Lighting a cigarette, he propped his heels on an old leather hassock. An old cop and a damn shrewd one.

Morely murmured, "I wouldn't mind a lengthy chat with Barada. And I'd like to know more about the Doc than I do. He's done time, by the way. Runs some kind of an herb store in Chicago now."

"Yeah, I ran credit traces on him."

Morely nodded musingly. "Any of the maids mention hearing a shot last night?"

"Not to me. There was only one floor maid working after eight last night. She was on change at the far end and unless Boyd was gunned in the hallway she couldn't have heard a shot."

"Neither did the neighbors," He sighed. "Spill me a little more java, Pete. I got a long dark night ahead."

Novak filled his cup and slid the brandy bottle across the table. Morely shook his head, "I can't waltz in singing *Sweet Barbara Allen*. Not that I wouldn't like to one night. There's a college-boy desk sergeant the captain dotes on, and the day I turn in my badge I'm busting his snotty nose for him."

"When's that?"

"Too damn long away." He drank the coffee steadily,

then lowered the empty cup. "I hear Barada's dame is a looker. Enough mink to stuff a trunk and a snappy little toy dog she sports around."

"Skye terrier."

"Maybe. Whenever I see a sub-rosa cutie like her I do the old-fashioned slow burn. If my wife's lucky this year she gets the old squirrel wrap reconditioned at Hecht's on a summer fur special. If we can't scrape up the dough she wears it another winter the way it is. But Boyd's kept woman can swirl into the Tilden in a cloud of silver mink and French perfume, never mind where the dough comes from or how." He shook his head disgustedly. "No wonder hoods figure police are squares. Hood kids get chauffeured cars to take them to private schools and riding academies; police kids hop a trolley or a crowded bus, rain, snow or shine. And carry their own lunches to save two bits each noon. But the public howls for a cop's blood when he takes a Christmas fiver from a bartender. They never figure the patrolman has been wrestling drunks out of the bar all year long and saving the mirrors and the furniture from getting busted. Some quiz genius grabs a hundred grand the clever way and the whole country dissolves in tears. Boo hoo. Ahhhhh, the hell with it. If I'm in the wrong game I've been in it too long to change." He stood up and reached for his hat. "Don't suppose you'd like to lend me your passkey so I could shake down the Doc's place. And the dame's?"

Novak got up. "Not without a search warrant, Lieutenant. It'd be my job. You know that."

"No harm asking."

"No harm."

He laid the crown of his hat in his right palm and squashed it on the top of his head. "The net's out for Barada, Pete. If you see him first, holler down the rain barrel."

Novak nodded.

"And thanks for the coffee and the California sauce."

"Any time." He followed Morely to the door, switched on the staircase light and waited until Morely was in the alley before turning it off. An honest, hard-working cop. Poor bastard. Within an hour he'd probably be following the meat wagon downtown to collect a throat-slit corpse; at three he might be poking around a Vermont Avenue rooming house, pulling prints off the windowsill of a room where an old lodger had been strangled by a prowl thief or rapist. And so on until well past dawn. With the Boyd murder still unsolved.

Novak loosened his tie, collected the used coffee gear and washed it in the kitchenette. Then he refilled the globe with water and measured coffee into the filter to save time in the morning.

He went into his bedroom, pulled off his shirt and shoes and lay down on the bed. For a while he smoked, thinking, and then he pulled over a half-finished cross-word puzzle from the Sunday supplement and filled a few more squares. "A dealer in textile fabrics" in six letters turned out to be *mercer*, a revelation which made him frown. Maybe the thing would flow from there.

The telephone rang and he lifted the receiver before

the ring had ended. It was a harsh gutter voice that spoke: "Novak—never mind who's talking. You been prowling around for some missing jewelry—well, I got it. What's the ante?"

"A grand was mentioned."

A hoarse guffaw. The voice sounded as though the man had a cold, as though his nose was stopped up. "Pal, that ain't even ten per cent."

"Five's the usual around Washington."

"Okay, five gees does it. Only it has to be tonight."

"Put aside the hop," Novak said. "Even if anyone was interested, who the hell could raise five gees at midnight? The stuff's insured. Get yourself a better deal with the company—Midland. In Chicago. They'll jump at the chance."

"Naw," the voice came back. "Long-distance calls are bad news anywhere. That makes it interstate and something for the G-boys."

"Maybe there's a local rep. Check the yellow pages and give them a buzz tomorrow."

"No interest, Novak?"

"A bare thimbleful."

Silence, while the line hummed indifferently.

"Make it three gees, then. And tonight."

"Look," Novak snarled, "I'm not in the old gold business, and I don't keep three, four thousand dollars in my sugar jar. If you made it five yards the answer'd still be no sale. I'll contact the party tomorrow, or if you're in a hurry, call her tonight. All she has to do is write a check. The hotel'll cash it."

"There's an idea," the voice mused. "Only suppose Fat Fanny rings the law?"

"That's the chance you take. And not a small one. If the stuff's too hot, mail it to the cops. Your problems couldn't interest me less."

The voice grew more urgent. "One grand, Novak. Last chance."

"For what?" he sneered. "Glory for old Pete Novak! No dice, pal. Fumble the merchandise yourself." He hung up, draped his legs over the side of the bed and lighted a cigarette. He could call Julia Boyd and tell her about the offer, or he could forget it. He could call Morely for the same reason, but Morely had only a secondary interest in the jewelry, and the chances were against its recovery providing any clues to the murderer.

That revived the question of whether the murderer and the theft were directly related. It was reasonable to assume that they were, but jewel thieves rarely drew blood. Of course the jewels could have come as a windfall after Boyd had been murdered. The caller didn't even have to be the original thief. He could have been a stage-one fence panicking on learning the murder connection.

Novak ran one hand through his hair, knocked ash into a tray and dialed the Tilden. He asked for Paula's room and waited until the operator had rung eight times. Then he hung up. Out on a midnight stroll, probably, or in a saloon huddle with her ex-husband.

He thought again about calling Morely and discarded the idea. Morely would have other things on his mind tonight. It was something to mention the next time they got together.

Beside him the telephone sounded. Automatically he reached for it and heard the voice of Julia Boyd.

She said, "I have just received a very interesting telephone call. And I was given to understand that the caller had phoned you as well."

"Possibly," Novak said. "What was the subject?"

"Stolen jewelry. The man said he had offered them to you for a price—a very low price—and that you had declined to become involved."

"That's an accurate summary," Novak said. "Anything else, Mrs. Boyd? These are the hours I try to dedicate to rest and freedom from worry. I told the man to get in touch with your insurance company, the police, or you."

"Novak, I want that jewelry back. I'll pay for it."

"How much?"

"Very little really. One thousand dollars. I have the sum in my room. But in my state of health I obviously am in no condition to venture out at night and deal with jewel robbers."

"And murderers."

"Oh? Yes. Of course there's that possibility."

Novak laughed shortly. "I like the casual way you finessed that, Mrs. Boyd. Yes, there's always that possibility, isn't there? I suppose you want your gems back and to hell with Chalmers's murderer."

Her voice grew frosty. "You know my attitude toward

Chalmers. He died painlessly, if I am to believe the police physician. Who killed him is a matter for the police to discover."

"Quite. Although you harbor your own suspicions."

"Indeed I do," she snapped. "I'm a stranger in this city. I know no one I can trust. That is why I am calling you. I have agreed to pay one thousand dollars for the return of my jewelry tonight. What is needed is a man to make contact with whoever has it, pay him and bring the jewelry to me."

"Tell the Doc. He's a good dark-alley type, and you seem to trust him."

"Doctor Bikel is not in his room," she said sharply; "therefore I am willing to pay you the sum I originally promised you for the return of the jewelry. One thousand dollars."

"We seem to get back to that same round figure. We keep batting it back and forth, and I haven't yet seen even a glimmer of green. A grand for me for running a simple errand? You wouldn't mind if I brought in a little police assistance, would you?"

"You can't," she protested. "That was part of the bargain."

"And you feel bound to treat thieves honorably."

"Listen, Novak, my ethics aren't under examination. I've got a job for you. It might take two hours of your time. In return I'm willing to pay you a thousand dollars."

"Cash," he said. "I get awfully weary of endorsing large checks."

"Very likely," she said coldly. "The instructions are for you to proceed to the corner of Connecticut Avenue and Bradley Lane—wherever that may be—leave your car there, and walk down Bradley Lane until contact is made."

"Yeah. One if by land and two if by sea. That's a pretty dark and deserted part of town this time of night."

"I didn't think you were short on courage."

"It comes and goes. Like a phony Harvard accent. What hour was mentioned, if I'm not too inquisitive?"

"Two o'clock."

"And the payoff money?"

"I'll seal it in an envelope and have it left at the desk for you. You can pick it up on your way out. I expect you to follow instructions implicitly and provoke no difficulties."

"Suppose they lift your money and neglect to give me anything in return?"

"It's a chance I'm willing to take. There isn't much time left. You may bring the jewelry to me in the morning. After nine o'clock." The line went dead, and Novak replaced the receiver slowly.

He thought for a while and then he dialed Police Headquarters and asked for Morely. The Lieutenant was out, the desk man told him. No telling when he'd get back. Where he was was police business. Novak left his name and hung up.

From a bureau drawer he took Paula Norton's chrome-plated pistol and slid it into his right hip

pocket. Then he fitted on his holster rig, spun the
cylinder of his .38 and stuck it loosely in the holster.

When he had laced his shoes he pulled on a coat,
got his hat and walked down the dark staircase to the
alley.

11

The envelope had been at the desk as Julia Boyd had said. Now it was in his right inside coat pocket. When he moved the steering wheel his arm brushed the envelope's slight bulge, reminding him of what lay ahead.

Connecticut Avenue traffic was scanty. A few cruising taxis, late trolleys rattling down the rails, and tourist cars with out-of-town licenses groping toward the center of the District. The black asphalt was slick with night dew, and he had to use the windshield wiper to clear off moisture.

Not a night to take long walks in the dark. He could have used some support from Morely, but the dice had rolled the other way. He wondered where Paula was. And Doc Bikel.

Chevy Chase Circle, with the bus station and the Chinese restaurant on the left. Now dark and inhospitable. Out of the District and into Maryland. Maryland, My Maryland. Let all the swains adore thee. Shoot if you must this old gray head, but spare your country's flag, she said. A highly unlikely incident. Eat Barbara Frietchie Bagels, Pretzels, Marmalade, and Crabburgers. Someone was coining dough off her old gray heroic head. American Enterprise.

Less than a mile to go. Not more. And no cars in a

long time. Only lighted diners and beer taverns and shy on business at that. Barbara Frietchie's Vitamin Pastrami will keep the teeth pegged in your jaw long after your neighbor's have dropped out.

The pistol in his hip pocket prodded naggingly. He shifted on the seat, found a new position. In the rear view mirror no trailing headlights, no car parked at the roadside ready to edge out and follow. Not even highway police. Hell, they'd be in a diner dunking crullers and cracking dusty jokes with a bored waitress. Seldom around when you needed them. Like obstetricians.

A sapphire ring, a diamond bracelet and an emerald brooch. Together they shouldn't make a parcel larger than a woman's fist. Concentrated wealth. Ninety thousand dollars worth. Sold for a thousand cash along a dark road. By someone who didn't have time to negotiate with the Midland Company. Someone who needed cash badly. Someone who would settle for a grand tonight in place of forty-five thousand next week. Not the most logical sort of deal. Unless the seller wasn't planning on turning over the jewels.

Only two more blocks to the intersection. Novak slowed the Pontiac, let it idle toward the curb. He turned off the ignition, dropped the key in his pocket and turned off the lights. A southbound truck zoomed past. Food for Washington's central market from the lush fields of southern Maryland. The dash clock showed ten minutes to two. His right hand slid inside his coat pocket, nudged the revolver and let it drop back into the holster. His license was good for the District, not Maryland. Now that he was over the line they could jug him for carrying concealed weapons. Two of them. He grinned at the darkness and got out of the car.

Locking it, he started up the road.

Streetlights flooded the intersection. He felt as conspicuous as a fly on vanilla icing. Not even the sound of traffic to cheer him. A lonely road, lighted at far intervals. Dark houses set far back from the road. Five minutes to two. Turning he looked back at the intersection. A car whizzed down Connecticut, taillights twin cigarettes in the darkness. Novak plodded on, stumbled on a stone and caught himself against a telephone pole. Ahead in the distant darkness the glow of headlights coming toward him. Novak moved farther to the right. The shoulder grass was high enough to wet his cuffs. He could hear the car's engine now coming at a measured, unhurried pace. He wondered if this was it.

It would be smart strategy to get him alone in headlights that could pick out any police covering him.

The car was closer now, only ten or twelve yards away. Novak strode along the shoulder, drainage ditch at his right. He could hear gravel crackle under the car's tires. Then a spotlight blinded him.

Novak covered his eyes with his left hand and kept walking.

He heard the car crunch to a stop. A voice barked, "Close enough. Let's have the dough."

"Let's have the jewels."

"This ain't your play, pal. Pull it out, and toss it over. Stay where you are. You're covered and plenty."

Novak drew the envelope from his pocket and sailed it at the car. It landed ten feet from the door. The door opened, someone got out, scooped up the envelope and got back in.

The spotlight went out and the voice snapped, "Here it comes."

Something sailed from the car window. Blinking, Novak snatched at it, let it land in the ditch behind him. Turning he knelt, grabbed his pencil flash and swiveled around. The beam cut through the darkness, illuminated the face of the driver.

The man's face twisted, the mouth gritted a curse, and the car spun away. A cloth was bound over the rear license plate.

There had been another man in the rear seat of the sedan, a man whose face he couldn't see. He had never seen the driver's face before, but he would remember it. The nostrils bulged grotesquely. They were packed with rolls of gauze to support the bridge of a broken nose.

Through the night came the squeal of tires as the car turned down Connecticut.

Novak played the light over the grassy ditch, reached down and brought back a roll of cloth tied with string. He stood up, brushed moisture from his knees, wiped sweat from his face and put the cloth roll into his coat pocket. Then he moved onto the road and began walking back toward Connecticut, whistling tunelessly as he went.

When he was behind the wheel he flicked on the map light and took the cloth roll from his pocket.

Untying the string he unrolled the cloth across his knees. Suddenly fire sparked through the car: green white and milky-blue. A bracelet, brooch and a ring.

Just like the man said.

He covered them carefully, separating each piece with a fold of cloth, and then he slid the roll into his pocket again.

Driving back into the District he stopped at a diner, ate a minute steak with French fries, a slab of peach pie and sloshed it down with black coffee. The cook rang up NO SALE, and took a dime from the register and dropped it in the counter tune selector. Fast pulsing jive flooded the diner. Novak wiped his mouth with a paper napkin, left money beside his plate and got back in his car.

He stayed on Connecticut as far as Massachusetts, turned down Sixth and drove over C as far as Police Headquarters.

Morely was typing a report when Novak went into his office. He glanced around and said, "You get up early these nights."

"I never really go to bed." Novak sat down in a wall chair, tilted it against the wall and watched Morely fill in and sign the last part of the report form. Morely got up, said, "Back in a minute," and took the report out of the office. Novak stared at the scarred desk, the tarnished spittoon, the chipped gooseneck lamp on the desk, and lighted a cigarette. After a while Morely came back.

"Not much of a place," he said sourly. "I always figured it's to keep us on the street and out of Headquarters." He sat down, lighted a half-smoked cigar and stared at Novak. "What'll it be, Pete?"

Novak leaned forward and laid the cloth roll on Morely's desk. Morely glanced at him and unrolled the cloth. Under the desk bulb the stones seemed to shine with life of their own. Morely raised his head slowly. "Jesus!"

Novak said nothing.

"How'd you come by them?"

"An hour or so after you left, a nameless voice called me. Said he had the jewelry and would trade it for five grand. I told him to lay off hophead schemes. We sparred back and forth, and I finally suggested he send the jewels to the police, the insurance company or Mrs. Boyd, their owner. Then I rang off."

Morely rolled the cigar slowly between his thumb and index finger. "Funny the guy'd call you."

"Thought so myself. Anyway, it wasn't long before Julia Boyd called with much the same story. The agreed price was one grand, with another for me when I return the stuff to her in the morning."

"So you went out and made the switch," he said unpleasantly. "With never a care in the world."

"I like money as well as the next fellow," Novak said evenly. "If you'd check your phone messages you'd find my name among them. It occurred to me you might like to have a lad or two nearby. To identify the sellers."

"Oh, you thought of that, did you?" Morely said a little wildly. "That shows great powers of reasoning.

But of course the switch couldn't wait until I could be found."

"I didn't make the arrangements, Lieutenant. Mrs. Boyd did. Leaving me with barely time to get to the rendezvous before the car showed up."

Morely restrained himself with difficulty. "Mind telling me what happened then?"

"That's why I'm here, Lieutenant. The time was two o'clock, the place, down Bradley Lane. Outside your jurisdiction, I might add."

"That makes me feel tons better," he said acidly. "Go on."

"Well, after I was a couple blocks from Connecticut —long blocks in the darkness, Lieutenant—this car came creeping toward me. When it was close it fanned a spot on me and a man told me to throw the money envelope at the car. When I'd done that they tossed this cloth roll at me. I let it go over my head, got down to look for it and put my pencil light on the driver's face."

Morely rubbed his hands together. "I was beginning not to like you. But you take chances, pal."

"A thousand dollars buys a few. Well, the driver had a damaged nose plugged with gauze. When he got the light on his face he got mad and drove away. Fast."

"Get the license number?" Morely had his pencil poised.

"Plate hidden by cloth. Dark blue sedan. Fifty-eight Chevy."

"Ever see the driver before?"

"No. But last night in the alley I kneed a guy in the face. His partner called him Tags."

"That's something," Morely mused. "Can't be too many hoods with that call-name. And you said Barada sent the two of them around. All out-of-towners probably."

Novak flicked cigarette ash at the spittoon, reached over and rolled up the jewelry.

Morely said, "Hey, that's material evidence."

"Of what, Lieutenant? Anybody find it at the scene of a crime? Anybody even know for sure it was ever there?"

"It had to be. Hell, look how you got it back. The guy who drilled Boyd copped them and sold them back."

Novak restored the cloth roll to his pocket. "That thought occurred to me, Lieutenant. It's so obvious that maybe we ought to sleep on it." He stood up. "Not many hours from now I may be richer by a thousand dollars. And you'll have only half as many things to look for. One murderer. Size and shape unknown."

Morely butted his dead cigar and wiped his face. "Barada gets more interesting by the hour. Think I'll ask the ex-wife where he can be reached."

"Think she'll tell you? If Barada's smart he's staying outside your jurisdiction. Even if you knew he was holed up, in, say, Maryland, you couldn't follow him across the line except in hot pursuit."

"Legally," Morely said thinly.

"We're talking legality. Hell, this is Police Headquarters. To do it legally you'd need a competent judge and damn near a writ of extradition. And you haven't got anything resembling grounds that any reasonable judge would listen to."

"Dream on," Morely said smoothly. "You finger him for me anywhere between the Pennsy border and South Carolina, and we'll see how much time I waste breaking a judge out of bed to keep things nice and legal. Judges are fine; some folks think they're even necessary. For me they're guys you tell the story to *after* all the action's over. And even then most of the bastards couldn't tell a crook from a Congressman."

"And that's not always easy. Any word from Winnetka on the late Chalmers Boyd?"

Morely lifted a sheet of yellow teletype. "Owned a bank, couple of loan companies and a factory that makes chemicals used in plastics. The name's here, but I can't pronounce it. Chamber of Commerce type, active in local charities—hell, you know those butter-and-egg men. More dough than sense. Paid his club bills on the day due, shot mid-eighty golf and had no known enemies. In short, a model citizen." He glanced up at Novak. "Except for the floozy he kept in Chicago."

"That make him unique?" Novak rattled the jewelry in his pocket. "I may sleep a little late in the morning, Lieutenant. Walking in the dark tends to tire me."

Morely shrugged, pulled a sheaf of papers from the corner of his desk and began looking through them. Novak went out the same way he had come.

In the hall he stopped at a pay phone and dialed the

Tilden. Paula's phone rang three times and then she answered sleepily. "Pete Novak," he said and heard a quick gasp of relief.

"Pete, what on earth....? It's after three o'clock. Don't you ever—?"

"Hardly ever. Called earlier but you were out. Thought I'd see if you got back. No problems?"

"No new ones. You were worried about me—is that why you called?"

"Uh-huh."

"I think that's rather nice, but good God, what a time to do it."

"I'll sleep better knowing you're sleeping well."

"And in my own bed."

"That, too. Oh, Lieutenant Morely may visit you in the morning. He'd like to get in touch with Ben Barada."

"I'll have to disappoint the Lieutenant. Ben checked out of that motel. For all I know he's gone back to Chicago."

"Even that much will interest him. We'll meet to-morrow, pumpkin."

He heard a kiss breathed close to the receiver, and then the line clicked off.

Novak walked down the echoing corridor and out into the night.

What little moon there was had come from behind the clouds, and there was a ring around it. Bad weather tomorrow. Or maybe just bad luck. He got into the Pontiac, started the engine and drove home.

12

The alarm broke him out at seven-thirty. For a little while he sat numbly on the edge of the bed, beating back an impulse to indulge himself in more sleep, then his mind began to function, reason took over, and he remembered the details of what he had to do.

The cold shower etched a plan in his mind. Toweling himself he turned on the coil under the coffeemaker and listened to the early news as he got dressed. Spring floods near Lancaster, plane crash at Richmond, a busty screen star married for the fourth time, some Congressman spouting on the German problem. Novak dunked the last piece of toast in his coffee, finished it and went down the staircase to a brilliant spring morning.

Instead of walking directly to the Tilden he cut over to Connecticut and went into a store. He was the only customer, and what he wanted took less than ten minutes. From there he strolled to K Street, crossed a nearly empty lobby and rode the elevator to the fifth floor.

Paula answered the door sulkily, and when he was inside she said, "God, what a nervous life you lead. Do you go without sleep entirely?" Knuckling her eyes, she turned and drew her dressing gown around her as she walked toward the sofa. "Don't mind me. I'm still in dreamland."

He shook out a cigarette, lighted it and gave it to her. Then he lighted one for himself and sat down in a chair. "I'd treat you to coffee," he said, "but I'd just as soon the help didn't know we were on intimate terms."

"For my reputation or yours?"

"Skip that one. I want to make this fast because Morely may be stopping by, and I wouldn't want him to think there was any collusion here."

Paula stretched her feet, yawned and said, "I'm listening."

Novak rested his cigarette on an ashtray and leaned forward. Slowly he told her what had happened the night before. As she listened her eyes widened, and the flesh seemed to shrink to the bones of her face. When he had finished she said, "You've given the jewelry back to Mrs. Boyd?"

He drew the cloth roll from his pocket and opened it on the sofa. She reached toward it, but he moved her hand aside. Quietly, he said, "Look like the real thing?"

"Of course." She stared at him. "Pete, let me have it. I can make a deal with her. There'll be plenty for both of us."

He shook his head slowly. "Sorry, beautiful. I take on only one customer at a time."

"You're crazy," she said quickly. "You'd let this go for a thousand when I could get you twenty."

"I'd be doing Ben Barada a favor. And I'm in the wrong mood for that."

"What would put you in the right mood?" she said suggestively.

He shrugged, reached out and rolled the cloth together. Then he put the roll in his pocket. Her eyes were still fixed on his face. "Small-time," she hissed.

Novak stood up, straightened his coat and looked down at her. "Guess so," he said. "And too old to change. I get scared when people talk big money to me. It scares me even when I don't believe it. So I'm taking this back to the only person who can legally claim it. Boyd's widow."

"Damn you," she said bitterly.

"Look at it another way. The stuff's hot. Any place it shows up except with the owner it'll cause trouble. Maybe you could fence it successfully, maybe not. You'd be using Barada's connections, and they could go sour awfully fast. He's a prime suspect in a murder case, remember? And however we split the proceeds he'd be getting his share from you. There's also the likelihood that you could be identified as the seller. Then there'd be a tidy circumstantial case against you as Boyd's killer." He butted his cigarette in the tray. Her eyes held a cold glint.

Novak said, "I'm glad you haven't a gun, sweetheart. The mood you're in I'd be lucky to leave in one piece."

"You said it, not me."

"Chances are you'll thank me one day."

"I doubt it like hell."

Novak laughed, turned and crossed to the door. Letting himself out he saw that she was still staring at him. "Don't bother to come back," she called harshly. Novak shrugged and closed the door.

Crossing the corridor he squared his shoulders and rang the bell. It was nearly nine o'clock, the time Julia Boyd had specified.

It took several rings to bring her to the door. Her hair was untidy, her face marked with sleep lines. She was still in her nightgown, a puffy, powdery bulk with large sagging breasts. As he followed her into the sitting room she said, "You're on time, I'll say that. Did you get it back?"

Opening the cloth on the coffee table he stood back. Julia Boyd reached for the bracelet first, pressed it lovingly to her breast, then fitted on the ring and admired the brooch in the light of the window. Turning she said throatily, "I'll get your money."

"I think I'd like a witness."

Her penciled eyebrows lifted questioningly. "What for?"

"Humor me, Julia. It wasn't a restful night."

"You're being paid for it," she snorted. "Witness to what?"

"That I returned the jewels to you. That you paid me for services rendered. Doc Bikel would do nicely."

Shrugging she laid down the jewelry and walked to the bedroom door. "Eddie," she barked, "come on out."

Novak grinned. "Wasting no time," he murmured and saw her angry glance.

Bikel trudged into the sitting room. He wore white pajamas piped in royal blue and his face was unhappy. When his eyes fixed on Novak his upper lip drew back over his teeth.

Julia Boyd said, "This man has brought my jewelry back to me, Eddie. He wants you to witness that fact. Why I don't know. I promised to pay him a thousand dollars for them." Her gaze turned toward Novak. "I don't have that much in cash here. You asked for cash as I remember."

Novak nodded. "A thousand dollars would just complicate my tax return, Mrs. Boyd. I'll settle for a yard— one hundred dollars. Ten percent of what you offered me."

Her eyebrows drew together. "You crazy?"

"Maybe. But basically I'm just a small-timer. In my world a hundred's what a thousand is in yours. Getting the jewels back took not over two hours of my time, and the risks weren't heavy. I'll settle for a hundred dollars."

Julia Boyd looked wonderingly at Bikel. "I wouldn't believe it if I hadn't heard it," she murmured and disappeared into the bedroom. She was rummaging through her purse when she came back. From it she took a fifty, two twenties and two fives. She laid them on the table beside the jewelry. Novak got up and went over to the writing table. On a sheet of hotel stationary he wrote: "I, Julia Boyd, acknowledge receipt of three pieces of jewelry from Mr. Novak, an employee of the Hotel Tilden, Washington, D.C. The items consist of a diamond bracelet, a sapphire ring and an emerald brooch. In consideration of his services I have rewarded Mr. Novak with the sum of one hundred dollars." Novak dated the statement and carried it over to Julia Boyd.

When she had read it she shrugged and passed it to Bikel. "See anything wrong with this, Ed?"

Bikel studied it carefully. He fingered his thin mustache, then shook his head. "Looks all right to me," he said uneasily.

Novak gave his pen to Julia Boyd who signed, followed by Bikel. Novak capped his pen, folded the statement into his wallet and picked up the bills. "Thanks, folks," he said. "You can hit the kip again. Sorry about the hour, but a hotel is a small city, and the trash collectors start pretty early."

Bikel smiled sardonically, toyed with the neck of his rumpled pajamas.

Novak grinned back. "One advantage in marrying Eddie is not having to change the initial on your linen." Then he turned and went out the door.

Crossing the corridor he punched Paula's button and waited until she called, "Who is it?"

"An old friend," he said. "Just wanted you to know she's got the rocks, and I've got a signed receipt. Witnessed by Bikel."

"Damn you," her voice came through the door.

"You said that before. Well, I wanted you to know that part's over. Tied up in satin. You can forget the jewelry the boyfriend unwisely lent you."

"Lent, nothing. It was a gift."

"Next time, get a bill of sale."

She swore at him. Novak left the door and walked on down the corridor.

Stopping in front of Bikel's room, he used his passkey and went in. The blinds were drawn, and the room was dark. Novak turned on the ceiling light and strode to the writing table. The Western Union pad was where he had last seen it. Peeling off the top sheet he carried it back to the door, went out and heard the spring lock click shut.

Back in his office he laid the telegram blank on his desk and took Julia Boyd's receipt from his wallet. He beckoned Mary over and showed it to her. When she had read it she gave it back to him. "How'd you manage that, Pete?"

"It's a fairly complicated story. One for a rainy afternoon and a thermos of coffee."

Mary went back to her desk. Novak folded the receipt into an envelope and dropped it in a safe drawer. Then he sat down at his desk and tilted the telegram blank under the desk lamp. He was reaching into a desk drawer for a brush and a bottle of graphite powder when the door opened and Lieutenant Morely came in.

Mary's typewriter was making little spattering sounds like hail on a cardboard roof. If they were still making roofs out of cardboard. As Morely advanced toward him Novak slid the telegram blank into the top drawer.

Morely's face showed a night's growth of beard, and his eyes were veined. Before he reached the desk Novak had the cigar box open. Morely took two and lighted one. When the end was glowing he said, "By God, you're a working man at that! Thought you planned an extra hour in the sack."

"Conscience booted me out. Busy night?"

"Two calls after you left. A bum hung hisself in Rock Creek Park, and an oyster boat fished a stiff out of the channel." He grinned. "Wow, nothing stinks like an old corpse."

"Or an unsolved murder."

"That, too." He knocked ash from the cigar. "Thought I'd check with you before I went up to see the Barada piece. Professional courtesy."

"I'd do the same for you. And she's calling herself by her professional name: Paula Norton."

Morely smiled lewdly, "What profession?"

"Give her a break if you can."

Morely whistled. "Must be quite a dame if she's gotten under your hide." He stood up. "She'll get all the breaks she's entitled to as a citizen. Nothing more. That's how we play it in the District."

"Unless she happened to be some Senator's sweetie. Don't feed me burnished morality so early in the day. Anyway, I can save you a trip. As of yesterday Barada was in the Vernon Motel this side of Alexandria—outside your jurisdiction. He's not there now."

Morely's eyes narrowed. "How the hell would you know all that?"

"She told me."

"And you held back the information from me?"

"I don't recall being asked the question."

Morely's face reddened. "I asked for your cooperation, Novak. I expected to get it. You say Barada's skipped out? Well, I'll remember how you helped him."

"You've gotten the cooperation you're entitled to as an officer of the law. That and nothing more—to quote your own words. I've got my own grudge against Barada, but I'd be glad to have you settle it for me. Where he was yesterday you couldn't touch him."

"And I've got a big fat chance of tracing him today." Morely's lips curled. "I'm not so crazy about you as I used to be. I didn't like the jewelry caper last night, and I like it even less right now."

"The widow's got it now. And there's no law against a person buying back his own stolen property. Insurance companies do it as a matter of course. If it was stolen."

"*If* it was stolen? What the hell's that supposed to mean?" Morely roared.

"Kick it around a little, Lieutenant. You have Julia Boyd's unsupported word that it was stolen. Nothing more. In legal terms I did her a favor last night. She's got her stuff back, and she's satisfied. I've got a signed receipt to prove it."

"And you let a possible murderer slip away in the darkness. Buddy, you got a funny way of looking at things." His voice was hard, his face taut with anger. "The hell with you, pal. I'm going to talk to Mrs. Barada, anyway. Maybe she'll be a little more helpful than you've been." He stormed out of the office.

Novak stood up and looked at his secretary. "Apparently I'm a son of a bitch," he said slowly.

"He didn't say so."

Novak shrugged. "The cops have a name for everything. Either you do the whole job for them or you're a dirty name." He shook his head. "Morely had a bad night. By the time he gets upstairs maybe he'll simmer down."

"I thought he was a friend of yours."

"Cops have no friends. The nature of the work's against it. They'll guzzle a beer with you, work out in the gym with you or shoot a round of practice targets, but that's as far as it goes. The world's full of thievery, bribery and violence. They can only hope to tackle a part of it. A few years on the job and they suspect everyone. Then they turn bitter. Talk to a cop's wife for an hour. Find out what kind of a home life she has."

Mary said nothing.

Novak walked past her, around the lobby wall and into the coffee shop. As he settled onto a stool Jerry came over, drew a glass of water and placed it in front of him. "Coffee, Pete?"

"Milk."

She studied his face and smiled. "Cranberry eyes. Okay, one milk coming up. Anything else?"

"Danish pastry and a few kind words."

She opened a carton of milk, poured it into a glass and cut a piece of pastry into small squares. Novak said, "You'd look pretty cute across a breakfast table, redhead."

"So they tell me." She rested her elbows on the counter and watched him eat. After a while she murmured, "You wouldn't look so bad yourself—after a night's sleep. Your job pay anything?"

"Practically nothing."

Her lips pursed and her head moved from side to side. "No sale. I could have gotten married when I was seventeen. The guy drops in here now and then. He's got a radio repair shop, a wife, four kids and more debts than he knows what to do with. My mother steered me out of that one, blessings on her grave. I figure a girl can only make one big mistake. I don't want mine to cost me a lifetime."

"Someone's got to marry the poor guys. Ever think of that?"

She stood back from the counter. "That's for someone else. Jerry's got other plans."

"Famous last words," he murmured and drank his milk. Jerry made a vixen face and moved down along the counter. Novak signed the check and crossed the lobby to the Assistant Manager's office.

Connery was wearing a pinstripe suit with a light blue shirt. There was a red carnation pinned on his lapel. When Novak came in he said, "Used Car Dealers' Convention next week. I've blocked eighty rooms for them. Plus the mezzanine reception room, banquet hall and the main ballroom for the last night. You may need some extra men for the night functions. Let me know how many before you go hiring them."

"Check."

"And make sure they look the part. Pressed tuxedos and clean cuffs and collars. We can do without more of your crummy waterfront pals."

"I'll march them in here to give them a look at a natty dresser. That do?"

Connery snorted. "Anything new on Boyd?"

"The cops haven't confided in me. One's up talking to Miss Norton right now."

"Who's she?"

"A friend from Chicago."

"Of the family?"

"She knew Boyd pretty well."

Connery's eyebrows lifted. He made a low whistle with his teeth. "So it's like that."

Novak lighted a cigarette, tossed the match in the wastebasket and gestured goodbye to Connery. After his discussion with Morely, he was in no mood for another inquisition.

He ambled out to the lobby and drifted from there through the dining room and the bar where waiters were readying for midday business, chatted with some of them and pushed through into the kitchen. He watched cooks adding ingredients to big aluminum kettles, then down to the laundry where women were feeding sheets through automatic ironers. A turn around the engine room, a friendly cup of coffee with the chief engineer and back up to his office.

Paula Norton was sitting in a chair near the reception desk. She was wearing a beige wool suit, matching pumps, a small crescent hat and gloves. When she saw Novak she got up and walked quickly toward him. Her eyes were wide, and her lips moved nervously. She put her hands on his arms and said excitedly, "Pete, the most wonderful news! While I was talking with that detective there was a long-distance call. From a lawyer in Winnetka—Chalmers's lawyer. Pete, Chalmers left a lot of money to me. The lawyer wants me to go to Winnetka right away." Her hands trembled with excitement.

"How much money?"

"He doesn't know yet—but it'll be plenty." She breathed deeply. "Half of the estate."

13

"Congratulations," Novak said stiffly.

Her face clouded. "Aren't you glad for me?"

"Delirious. Working girl makes good. You worked for it, too."

Her hands dropped away, her lips quivered slightly. "You're damn right I worked for it!"

"Let's hope you get it. Only don't think the widow will give it up without a fight."

"Let her try," she flared, then her eyes narrowed. "What could she do?"

"Charge undue influence, among other things. Judges and juries are pretty conservative, beautiful. I'd guess they'd take a poor view of a solid citizen depriving his wife of anything in favor of an after-hours cutie. So long, gorgeous. See you in the headlines." He moved past her, but one hand held him.

"Damn you. You'd love to see that happen."

Turning he faced her. "Hell, you're worse off than ever. We cleaned up the jewelry problem, but another motive's cropped up. One the police won't be likely to ignore. And Julia will be in there every minute, pitching and batting out the whole arsenal of legal and wifely tricks. If you get anything after the smoke's cleared away, you'll *really* have earned it."

"Any more advice?" she said tightly.

"Don't spend the dough until you've got it." He laughed shortly. "That's good advice for anyone."

Her chin lifted and her eyes surveyed him. "What a cheap little world you live in. Nickels and dimes and two weeks' vacation a year. How much are you charging me for the other night?"

"For bringing romance into your life?"

She flushed quickly. "For removing a body."

"Half of anything you get," he said coolly.

She stepped back and crossed her arms. "That would be about right, wouldn't it? But you can't prove anything. Only you and I know he was ever there."

"And the murderer."

She bit her lower lip. Then she snapped, "He won't be telling anybody. But I'll pay you, Novak. I wouldn't be under obligation to you for the world."

"That's a fast reverse. Not long ago you were grateful beyond words. Now I've got a claim if I can prove it. Well, don't bother. Long ago I charged it off to charity."

Paula spun around and half-ran toward the doorway. A few eyes stared at Novak. Wetting dry lips he reached for a cigarette, found the pack empty, crumpled it into an ashtray and strode toward the cigar counter.

A short fat man was kidding the girl behind the counter. When she saw Novak she moved quickly to the cash register, rang up the sale and pressed change into the man's hand. He opened his mouth to say something, but she had already forgotten him. His mouth clamped shut, and he walked huffily away. She slid a package of cigarettes across the counter to Novak and added a pack of matches. He gave her half a dollar and said, "Didn't mean to break up anything."

"Those old goats never give up, and all the young, good-looking guys are married." She smiled sexily. "Most of them anyway."

Novak opened the package, extracted a cigarette and lighted it. "Don't mind me, Sylvia," he said dully. "I'm not myself these days."

"You don't even look like yourself. Where'd you spend the night? On a coal barge?"

"Wish I had," he said moodily. "I'd feel less frayed." Resting one elbow on the counter he blew smoke at the paperback rack.

Sylvia said, "I've been thinking about that cup of schnapps you mentioned. It just happens I haven't a thing to do tonight except brush my hair and watch TV."

Novak reached for a postcard and took out his pen. He scribbled on the slick card and handed it to her. "Address and phone number. We might even improve on the schnapps. Any time after eight."

"Make mine bourbon," she said throatily. "Mixed or straight. How do you like your breakfast eggs?"

"Over easy. And a rasher of bacon." He saw Connery crossing the lobby and moved away from the counter. As he glanced back she blew him a kiss.

Novak turned around in time to see a man moving hurriedly toward the street door. Doctor Edward Bikel in a dark topcoat and dark hat. Bikel pushed through the revolving doorway almost knocking down an incoming bellhop. The hop dropped the bags and gave

Bikel's back a redfaced glare. Then he jerked up the bags and trudged toward the reception desk. Behind him followed two chesty ladies in tweed coats and sensible shoes. Career travelers on their husbands' insurance money, and fond of cream sherry and English cigarettes.

His eyes returned to Bikel who was fitting himself into a taxi.

Novak walked through the doorway, waited until Bikel's cab had pulled away and made a sign at the doorman. The lead cab ground up, and the doorman opened the door. Novak got inside and said, "Follow that cab."

The driver half-turned and sneered, "Give me a reason, buddy."

"The reason is I'm the hotel security man, and I'm asking for some quiet cooperation."

The driver's foot hit the accelerator and the taxi leaped ahead. "Cripes," he complained. "I was only asking. This here's a screwy town. That's Al Fornella's cab, and we're on him like bumper tape."

Novak sat back and stubbed his cigarette in the ashtray. The cab stayed on K Street, rounded the public library, passed the market and stayed on K another four blocks. At First Street the cab turned and drove north past Armstrong Tech.

The driver said, "He's slowing. What do I do now?"

Novak sat forward. Bikel's cab was making for the curb a block ahead. "Pass him, and go around the block. I want to spot where the fare goes."

Bikel was getting out. He hurried up a walk that led

to an old red brick house. As Novak went by he saw
a flaked wooden sign over the porch steps: HOTEL
JENSEN. GUESTS BY DAY, WEEK OR MONTH. Bikel
jogged up the steps and opened the screen door. The
waiting cab's flag was still down. The driver was bent
over, tuning the radio.

Novak's cab went around the block slowly. As it came
back onto First Street, Bikel's cab pulled away. Framed
in the rear window was the back of Bikel's head. The
driver said, "What now?"

"Let me out at the Jensen." He read the meter, got
out the fare and added a dollar. As the cab stopped
Novak handed it to the driver.

"Thanks. Say, that's okay. Any time, pal."

"The name's Novak." He got out and walked up the
sidewalk.

A four-story brick house old enough to have ten-
foot bow windows and crenellated balconies, set far
back from the street under tall elms that had won a
stand-off battle with a scanty lawn. Roots lifted the
walk unevenly, and dry rot had made away with most
of the bannister supports along the front steps. Dusty
windows deflected filtering sunlight, and the stillness
made Novak tread lightly as he crossed the wooden
porch.

Inside the door was a reception counter with a punch
bell and a length of inkstained blotter. The curling cal-
endar on the wall advertised a patent cough medicine.
In better days it had been a reception hall where servants greeted guests and helped with their cloaks. The
flowered hall-runner was worn down almost to burlap.

At the far end there was a carved door with frosted glass panels. The door was partly open, and from the opening there peered a white-thatched head. Nothing more. The face was pale and wrinkled with surplus flesh. A pince-nez bridged the thin nose, a satin ribbon trailing away behind the door, it was a face so old as to be almost sexless, except for the way the white hair was parted and combed.

The door opened a little further, and Novak saw trousers, white suspenders and a striped, collarless shirt. Slippered feet shuffled toward Novak, and the voice piped, "We have a nice vacancy, young man. Two dollars a night. But for a week or more we could offer a nice discount. Would you care to see it?"

"I'm sorry. Dr. Bikel asked me to meet him here. I'm a little late so perhaps he's already arrived."

Disappointment gnawed the bloodless lips. "I...I don't believe I know a person by that name."

"Tall and thin. Wears glasses and dark clothes, also a pencil mustache." Not much of a word picture, Novak thought as the old man shuffled closer.

Light spread downward from the old eyes. "That must be Dr. Barnes. Such a nice man. So very pleasant. Considerate, too. Yes, that would be Dr. Barnes. From out of town." One finger tapped his lower lip. "Dr. Barnes arrived not long ago. But I believe I heard the door close. So he must have left."

"Or it could have been me coming in," Novak said helpfully. "I'll just go on up and see if he isn't there. What was the room number?" His face formed a frown of concentration.

The old man blinked and stared at Novak uneasily. Bothered by failing memory, probably. Wasn't sure of the day or the month. A perfect place for Bikel.

The old man said, "The room is Number Four. Just walk up the stairway, and follow the hall down to the far end. At the back. It's really quiet easy to find. All of our rooms are numbered. Number Four is a nice room. For Dr. Barnes we made a special rate—he being a medical man and all."

"A credit to his profession," Novak murmured and began walking up the long stairway.

At the jog there was a tall window of colored glass in an old-fashioned geometric design. Falling sunlight spattered the risers with red, green and yellow in a senseless pattern. It stained Novak's shoes as he trod the steps to the hallway.

There was a grimy chandelier suspended by a tarnished gilt cable, and spaced along the hall were blackened gas pipes mounted with dusty glass mantels. An old, old house, relic of a far more gracious age.

The flooring was grimed oak, partly covered with cheap carpeting in a somber shade. Brass-plate house numbers had been nailed to room doors. As the old man had said, Number Four was the farthest down the hall.

Through one of the doors drifted a ragged, rubbing sound. Novak decided someone was scrubbing clothing on a basin washboard. He moved on and stopped in front of the door with 4 tacked onto a center panel. For a moment he listened, heard nothing, then knocked.

The lock must have failed to catch, because the rap

of his knuckles moved the door inward. It opened far enough to show speckles of light slanting into the room through a tattered roll curtain. There was a brown bureau with peeling veneer, a washbasin with a small wooden mirror cabinet above it, two chairs and an iron bed.

The bed had chipped, yellow enamel with vertical rods at the end to hold the mattress in place. The bed-spread had faded stripes, and it was rumpled from the body beneath.

She lay on her right side, arm under her head and projecting stiffly beyond the mattress. The fingers were curled slightly as though death had halted a reaching movement.

Novak felt for the wall switch and turned on the bulb.

Even without her glasses he could recognize her. She was the woman who had run from Bikel's room, the woman he had followed to the chapel. Her eyes were closed, and her lips were parted. The skin of her face looked as if it had been washed with light blue dye.

Join the fellowship of prayer, he thought, and stepped closer to the bed. Bending over he touched the dead hand and drew back. Rigor mortis…hours dead. Turning he walked to the wash basin. The flat edge held an empty water glass. Beside it stood an open brown bottle labeled *Keep Away from Children*. Peering into it he could see that whatever it might have held, it was empty now.

His body was chilled. He moved stiffly toward the bureau and opened the top drawer. Nothing there except her glasses. Nothing in the other four drawers either. In the closet a cheap fiber suitcase lay open. It held a disarranged dress, a pair of shoes and some cheap stockings and underwear. Nothing more.

Novak went back to the bed, pulled down the covers and stared at the body's left hand. The third finger held a plain gold wedding band, not new. He rearranged the covers and stared around the room. Yesterday the little woman had carried a handbag. Now there was no trace of it. The bag would have held cards, a driver's license, perhaps, or a Social Security card. Without them there was no easy way of identifying her.

Turning off the wall light he felt death hovering close, like a smothering fog. He went out of the doorway leaving the door as he had found it, walked quietly along the hall and down the stairway.

The old man was sitting in a rocker, eyes closed, chin on his chest, sleeping the shallow sleep of the very old.

Novak went behind the counter and opened the thick registration ledger. The cover was bound in frayed blue buckram, corners worn down to the original cardboard. Novak thumbed the wide pages until he found a place where a page had been torn out. The registrations ended the month before. Closing the book he moved softly to the door, opened it carefully and went out to the porch. Bikel hadn't missed a trick. He'd taken the handbag and the identifying registration as well.

Novak's throat was tight, constricted. He moistened his lips and gulped a deep breath as the steps creaked under his weight. Then down the uneven walk, past patches of starving grass and out to the street. He walked south as far as a sagging grocery store and stepped into a phone booth. The tattered directory gave him Police Headquarters, and when the duty sergeant answered Novak said, "First Street, the Jensen Hotel. Room Four."

"Yeah? What's your name? And what's in the room?"

"A corpse," Novak rasped and hung up.

Near Armstrong Tech there was a cab stand. Novak got into one and rode back to the hotel.

From the house phone he called Bikel's room, let the phone ring a long time and hung up. Then he went into his office. His secretary was at the file safe checking names. Novak slid behind his desk, turned on the lamp and opened the center drawer. He laid the telegram blank on the blotter and got out the bottle of graphite powder and a small camel's hair brush. Working carefully he distributed the fine black powder over the surface of the blank, brushed gently and blew away the surplus. Where there had been nothing but blank impressions, block letters had formed. Most of the message was legible, including the address.

Mary was looking over his shoulder. "Reading other people's mail?"

"I had to." He slid the developed message into his desk drawer and locked it. Mary said, "Must be important."

"Evidence." He reached into a lower drawer, felt for the bottle and set it on the blotter. Unscrewing the cap he lifted the bottle and let a good two ounces wash down his gullet. Then he capped the pint and put it back in the drawer. Mary said, "I don't see how you can drink it like that—without water or ice or anything."

"You get used to it."

She snorted disapprovingly and went back to the card files.

Novak loosened his collar, stared around the room. It was clean at least, and reasonably comfortable. Not like the flophouse where the little woman had gasped out her life. Closing his eyes he saw again the speckles of light across the rumpled bed, the hook of her hand, the spittle-covered blue lips and the empty brown bottle. He rubbed the edge of one hand over his eyelids and opened them. It was a scene to forget, not one to engrave in your memory. He shivered, reached for the box of goodwill cigars and bit the end from one. The door opened, and Connery came into the office. He walked rapidly to Novak's desk and sat down opposite him. He pushed a banquet plan across the desk, and then his nostrils quivered. He sniffed, and his lips pursed. "You've got a whisky breath," he said accusingly.

Novak lighted the cigar, drew in and blew smoke across the desk. Connery coughed and drew back. Novak smiled winningly. "What'll we do about it, Ralph? Give me the balloon test?"

Connery jumped up, fanning cigar smoke aside. "A roughneck like you has no place in a refined hotel like this," he shouted. "I'm going to take it up with the Manager."

Novak smiled. "Okay. But the Manager knows damn

well I've saved his job on at least two occasions. Now what about the banquet?"

Connery whirled and darted out of the office. As the door closed Mary turned and said, "I'd hate to lose you as a boss, Pete. Can't you go easy on Connery? Or was it true what you said about the Manager?"

"Not entirely," Novak said calmly. "Last year he had a floozy stashed away in a room on the sixth floor, and the hotel wasn't collecting any rent. We had a quiet talk, and the lady agreed to move out of the low-rent district. So don't worry about Connery busting my corset stays. When I quit it'll be because I'm sick of the place."

Jimmy Grant hustled in, glanced nervously at Mary and went to Novak's desk. Leaning over he said in a low voice, "She checked out, Pete. The Norton dish."

Novak said nothing. His eyes had narrowed, staring at a letter opener on his desk.

Jimmy said, "You wanted to know, didn't you?" He sounded crestfallen.

Rousing himself Novak pulled over the phone.

"Yeah," he said huskily. "I wanted to know."

Then he dialed Police Headquarters.

14

Novak ate lunch in the coffee shop and spent a couple of hours going over the hotel with a fire inspector on a periodic inspection tour. When the inspector left, Novak turned back from the front entrance and started walking to his office. As he neared the reception counter he saw the clerk beckoning at him. "May I trouble you a moment, Mr. Novak?" he chirped.

Novak angled over and saw a man resting an elbow on the marble counter. He wore a houndstooth coat, flannel slacks, moccasin shoes and a stitched-brim tweed hat. His green challis tie was figured with trout flies, mostly concealed by a beige corduroy vest. A very sporty customer, Novak decided and looked at the face.

It was a face that would have been overly handsome but for a nose bridge that might have been broken and set repeatedly. As Novak neared him, the man's elbow left the counter, and he straightened the lapels of his coat. The shoulders had the powerful roll of an athlete, and the eyes that surveyed Novak were cool and steady. To Novak he looked like a man who had seen the collegiate light-heavyweight ring within the last ten years.

Novak laid one hand on the counter and looked at

the clerk. The clerk coughed nervously. "This gentleman was inquiring for someone, Mr. Novak. I thought you might be able to provide the information."

Novak turned his glance to the other man.

The man reached a gloved hand into his coat, extracted an ostrich wallet and selected a card. He gave it to Novak and put away the wallet. The card was good quality stock, engraved with a name: Pike Hammond, St. Louis. There was a telephone number over the lower right-hand edge. Novak dropped the card in his pocket, said, "What was it you wanted, Mr. Hammond?"

The man's smile was casual. He spread his gloved hands and said, "Looking for an old friend. Seems I may have missed her. The clerk thought you might have more information."

"Who's the friend?"

Almost indifferently the man said, "Name of Barada —but I understand she's using her maiden name, Norton."

"Miss Norton checked out before noon."

Hammond nodded. "It occurred to me she might have left a forwarding address."

Novak gave the clerk a long stare. The clerk swallowed hard and fluttered away. Then Novak said, "She left no forwarding address, but something was mentioned about Winnetka, Illinois. Too bad you missed her, Mr. Hammond."

He shrugged. "That's how the ball bounces." His eyes moved over Novak. "She stayed here alone?"

"Single reservation."

"Too bad," he said musingly. "Thought I might be able to connect up with her husband. Actually he's the one I needed to see."

Novak drummed his nails on the counter. "What's your line of business, Mr. Hammond?"

The man's lips pursed slightly, then resumed their even smile. "We could call it the entertainment business," he said smoothly. "How's that sound?"

"Passable," Novak said. "Which end, Mr. Hammond?"

Hammond's smile showed white, sturdy teeth. "The collection end. But we weren't talking about me."

"Excuse the detour. Where'd you know Ben Barada? Northeast Illinois?"

"Chicago?"

"I was thinking of Joliet."

The smile thinned. "A fellow like Big Ben does a lot of traveling. In the course of a year you could spot him in twenty or thirty places: Hialeah, Hot Springs, New Orleans, Vegas…"

"And St. Louis."

"Wherever the fast money moves." One hand made a fist and hit the gloved palm of his other hand. "Time's a-wasting," he remarked. "Thanks, fella. This has been a big disappointment." He started to move past Novak. Novak's elbow blocked him.

"Down, boy," Hammond said icily. "Playtime's over."

"Relax," Novak said. "You've come a long way to see Barada. No need to go away thirsty."

Hammond's eyebrows lifted. "I'm not a drinking man," he said, "but I don't object on principle."

Novak took his arm and steered him into the bar.

They sat on a curved corner seat and ordered Irish and a Coke. Hammond took off the tweed hat and smoothed dark brown hair. Just above the hairline there was a white scar that could have been a bullet crease. He pulled off his gloves slowly, and Novak saw the battered knuckles of a fighter. The gloves were Italian peccary at about thirty bucks a pair.

Hammond waited until Novak had lighted a cigarette and said, "You've got quite a line on old Ben. How come?"

"He got into trouble a couple of nights ago."

Hammond eased forward. "What kind of trouble?"

"Slapping his wife around."

Hammond picked a wooden match from the ashtray box and rubbed one end against an upper incisor. "You blew the whistle?"

Novak nodded.

Hammond smiled unevenly. Novak lifted his right elbow and eased it casually against Hammond's coat. There was something hard and bulky under the well-tailored houndstooth. Hammond's eyes flickered. "Yeah," he said. "I'm rodded. So what?"

"I like to know what I'm talking to," Novak said. "Sorry about the crude frisk." He took his glass from the waiter and waited while Hammond's Coke was poured. Hammond wet his lips and lowered the glass slowly. "I got a thing on about guys who beat up dames," he said harshly. "Barada would be about right for that —on top of everything else."

Novak sipped some of his drink and knocked ash from his cigarette. "Ben was padded outside town, on the road to Alexandria. A motel called the Vernon. You could maybe pick him up from there, but I doubt it."

"Anyone try?"

"The police maybe."

Hammond's face paled slightly. "I don't like that. Ben can't afford to mix with the coppers. Not now. Not until we finish a little business matter. After that he's up for grabs." He swallowed some Coke and stared at Novak. "Any chance he headed for Winnetka with Paula?"

"It's possible. She's lately been remembered in a rich man's will. She seems to think she owes something to Ben. He may have gone along to protect her interests—and his own."

"What rich man?"

"Fellow name of Boyd. Died here the other night."

Hammond nodded reminiscently. "Paula's sugar-daddy. Yeah, I heard of Boyd before. From Ben. She was to put the bite on Boyd and Ben was to have his cut by yesterday. When he didn't call the boss, I caught a plane east." He stared at the end of Novak's cigarette. "The boss is holding a fistful of worthless paper. If he lets Ben get away with it, other guys will try and I'll be busier than I like." He picked up his glass, finished the Coke. "Used to be Ben signed an IOU and made it good next morning when the banks opened. Maybe Joliet sours a guy. I imagine it could."

"How much paper did Ben leave behind?"

"Sixty-five grand. Too much to write off with a grin. And the boss rarely grins." He glanced down at a thin gold wristwatch. "Think I'll hire a car and drive out to the motel. I might just get lucky." Pulling a bill from his pocket he covered the check and stood up. "I never did business with a hotel peeper before. And not even a harsh word."

Novak looked up at him. "What business?" he asked and saw Hammond move away toward the bar door.

No wonder Barada had been frantic to get his hands on a chunk of money. A guy like Hammond could pick him up and bang him against a wall until his toenails dropped off. Novak took Hammond's card from his pocket and studied it. Discreet and tasteful. Telling nothing. A name and a telephone number. Like a high-price bordello.

Novak fitted the card into his wallet, finished his drink and left the bar. Crossing the corner of the lobby he went out to the sidewalk and waited while the doorman helped a woman from a cab. Then he went over to him and said, "Art, not long before noon a Miss Norton checked out. Gray fur, gray luggage and maybe a small dog on a gray leash."

"No dog," Art said, brushing lint from the sleeve of his coat. "I'd remember her anyway because she didn't take a cab. There was a car waiting for her. Couple of guys in it. She got in, and they drove away."

"What kind of a car?"

"It was new enough to be rental. I didn't pay much attention to the plate numbers, but it was a District plate." He squinted at Novak. "She skip?"

Novak shook his head. "A fellow was asking for her," he said and walked slowly back into the hotel. Crossing to the reservation desk he went behind it and motioned the girl away from the teletype. Sitting down he selected the line to the chain's St. Louis hotel, consulted Hammond's card and tapped out a message. He tore off the yellow teletype sheet and carried the message toward his office. In an hour or so there ought to be an answer.

Over at the tobacco stand a newsie was unloading a pile of afternoon papers. Novak bought one and went back to his office.

The Jensen Hotel death rated a paragraph on page fourteen, just ahead of the classifieds. Only the bare facts. An unidentified middle-aged woman had been found dead in her room. Death was due to either heart failure or an overdose of sleeping pills. A brief description of the woman followed, plus a police request for any information that could assist identification.

Novak tore out the clipping and laid it in his desk drawer. Beside the dusted telegram blank. Then he skimmed the rest of the paper and tossed it into the wastebasket.

Mary said, "How'd the fire inspection go?"

"We're certified for another month." He wrote a name on a pad and carried the slip over to Mary. "Not a bad guy. Put him on the Santa Claus List. Two turkeys and a large basket of fruit. Gift-wrapped."

She made a shorthand note under the man's name. "Wouldn't mind one myself."

"He's got four kids," Novak said. "The chain can afford it and a lot more. I wouldn't like to try to feed a family of six on what a fire inspector draws from the District."

"No," she said soberly. "You sound a little mellower today. Any special reason?"

"I just had a drink with a bill collector. I guess there's tougher jobs than mine."

"I should think so. Bill collectors work on a percentage, don't they?"

"The house percentage. And the house always wins." He laid the teletype message on her desk. When she had read it she glanced up. "*That* kind of a bill collector," she said breathily.

"With the trouble boys there's not a live case of failure to collect. This one's so tough he doesn't have to strut to prove it. Very cool and silky and muscled like a bull gorilla. College education, by his grammar, and probably knows what spoon to use. The rackets don't pick their personnel off the cattle boats any longer. It's big business now, and the accent's on brains. Congress and TV have given old-fashioned hoodlums a negative public image, so the syndicates employ muscles that can pass in a crowd without old ladies shrieking and fainting away." He walked back to his desk and sat down. "The law tries to compete, but the pay's too low. Competent prosecutors are playing to the voting public, and their working assistants are kids just out of law school who couldn't connect with an established firm. Not much competition against the talent the syndicates can afford to hire. Hell, there's hardly a big law firm in the East without one or more syndicate clients."

"You don't see their names in the papers. The law firms, I mean."

"They work those things out over brandy at the club with the guys who own the newspapers," he said tiredly. "Besides, the prosecutors are so busy grabbing space that when a defense attorney isn't highlighted, nobody notices. The best people," he said sourly. "Ah, the hell with them."

The office door opened, and Lieutenant Morely came in. He nodded at Mary, took off his hat and sat down near Novak. He was shaved, but his eyes were reddened, and his face looked haggard. He said, "Thanks for the tip on Paula Norton. Unfortunately she hasn't been located yet." He sat forward and smiled thinly. "You fooled me, boy. I thought you was maybe sweet on her, and here you turned her in like a little soldier."

"All in the spirit of cooperation."

Morely leered at him. "I'll bet. The truth is she probably wouldn't lay for you, and you got sore."

Novak's hand shot out and jerked Morely's tie forward. "Little plump pal," he snarled, "who lays for me and who doesn't isn't a matter for police speculation." His fingers released the tie and Morely's flushed face bobbed up. Novak's fist tapped Morley's chin lightly. "The lady checked out. I notified the police as requested. Leave it at that, Lieutenant."

Morely's right hand had gone for his belt gun, but it stopped short, the fingers opened and closed stiffly, a nerve fluttered in his mottled face. Slowly the back of his hand ran across his lips, fingers straightened his knotted tie. "Jesus, you take chances," he said hoarsely. "Last guy who did that ain't around to tell it."

"I'm chilled to the bone." Novak bit off the words. "You were just kidding, and I'm edgy today. Want to write it off?"

Morely was sitting deep in his chair, hands flat on his thighs, eyes staring at Novak. After a while he said, "Hell, I didn't know you were so touchy."

Novak got out the box of hotel cigars. Morely took two and stuck them in his coat pocket without looking at them. The color of his face was nearly normal. His voice was still unsteady when he spoke: "We got a call from Mrs. Boyd. All upset and bitter. She wanted someone to come right over and arrest Norton for murdering her husband. By then we'd got your message, and when they told her Norton had checked out she yelled and foamed at the muzzle."

"What kind of evidence was she suggesting you arrest Norton on?"

"Said she had detective agency reports that they were lovers." He made a sound of disgust. "If we arrested every dame who was kept by a married guy we'd have jails in every block." He heaved a long sigh. "I stopped by Bikel's room before coming here, wanted to get a detailed account of his movements the night Boyd was shot. But he wasn't around."

"Maybe Julia could find him."

"Maybe. And I'd just as soon not be the one to ask her. She treats policemen like wetbacks, and I haven't slapped a dame in a couple of years. Yeah, Bikel's an interesting fellow. You said they were planning to kneel at the altar?"

"They're already bundling."

Morely's eyebrows lifted. "How would you know that?"

"They were in pajamas when I went up to her suite this morning."

Morely chuckled lecherously. "Some guys will do anything for dough. But of course Bikel couldn't marry her so long as her husband was alive. Yeah," he said thoughtfully, "I sure want a long interview with Doctor Edward Bikel."

"Boyd wasn't the only obstacle." Novak opened his drawer and took out the newspaper clipping. He reached it over to Morely who read it and handed it back, shaking his head. "An old dame conks out in a fleabag hotel—so what's that got to do with the business at hand?"

Novak pulled out the dusted telegram and laid it under the desk lamp. Morely got up and peered down at the block letters. Then his face lifted slowly. "What's the connection?"

"Yesterday I saw a woman answering the newspaper description run from Bikel's room. I was close enough so that I could hear they'd been having emotional words. When I got the chance I shook down Bikel's room and pulled this off the top of the telegram pad."

Morely scanned the message again. "There doesn't have to be a connection," he said slowly.

"Checking's easy. He sent this to a Mrs. Edward Bikel in Chicago at the address given. The message tells her not to come to Washington and spoil everything. It promises he'll work everything out and be back in a few days." Novak lighted a cigarette and let smoke drift over the desk. "You could call Chicago and see if Bikel's wife is at this address, or if not where she's gone. It's worth the try, anyway. And there ought to be somebody around the neighborhood who could give you a description of Mrs. Edward Bikel." He lifted the clipping and let it flutter onto the desk. "If the dead woman and Mrs. Bikel turn out to be the same person, the Doc might have to postpone his wedding."

"Yeah," Morely growled, "while we sweat the truth out of the son of a bitch."

15

Mary had gone home, and except for the light on Novak's desk the office was dark. The blinds were partly open, showing moving forms hurrying along the sidewalk. Through spaces between people he could glimpse the slow crawl of traffic. The windows were closed and what sounds penetrated were muffled and detached. He had been smoking in the near darkness, isolated and alone, sipping Irish whisky and turning things over in his mind.

In the lobby it was the time after the check-out hour bustle and before the evening business began. The time when the help changed shifts, when the dining room opened and the muted sounds of the string trio drifted through the hotel. No raucous page boy bellowing the name of an out-of-town visitor. No slurred chatter of idle women leaving the cocktail lounge. No slapping of convention hands on convention backs or shouts of merry recognition. No drunks fighting the potted palms. All that came later. For now everything was hushed, suspended. Waiting for the night to come.

His head tilted back, and he stared at the shadowed ceiling. A hotel is like a prison, he thought. The rooms are cells hiding secrets and passions. Then something happens, the smallest thing, and doors fly open. The explosion goes off. Panic. And fragments of truth.

He shook himself, forced his eyes to the empty desk. He began to think about Paula, wondering where she was. He thought of the teletype from the St. Louis house security man and wondered if Pike Hammond had found the trail of Ben Barada. Hammond and the boss who seldom smiled.

He picked up the long steel letter opener, toyed with it. The end stabbed little nicks in the smooth green blotter. He wondered if Morely had found Bikel and what their talk had disclosed. He thought of a horrid old fat woman in a fifth-floor suite and wondered what was on her devious mind.

Stubbing out his cigarette he got up heavily and pulled on his coat. One hand buttoned his collar, slid the tie knot into place. The pint bottle was empty. He dropped it in the wastebasket and heard it bounce against the metal sides. Then he turned off his desk lamp and went out.

A few guests reading newspapers in the lobby. A couple in evening dress left an elevator and strode sedately to the revolving door. Another girl behind the tobacco counter. Sylvia would be home now, fixing dinner for her kid and thinking about things she had to do before eight o'clock. Tough being a divorcée with a kid to care for. Maybe it was tougher staying married to a man who cheated on you or drank too much or couldn't hold a job. Or beat you up for laughs. Like Ben Barada. I don't know which is tougher, he said to himself. I've got only the male angle, but it's not always the woman who cops the raw deal.

He walked slowly toward the elevators and the bell captain came over to him. "Bikel hasn't showed, Pete. Everybody's got the word. If he comes in we'll spot him."

"Thanks, Andy." He stepped into the open elevator and said, "Five."

The doors hummed shut, the cage lifted smoothly on its purring cable.

As the doors opened the operator said, "Everything okay, Pete?"

"Everything's okay." He walked down the hall and turned into the corridor. There was a light in the service closet, a maid fussing inside. As he walked he could see the luggage dolly leaning where he had left it after transferring Boyd's corpse. Only two nights ago? It seemed like half a year. His head was buzzing. He stopped, shook himself, walked on. Too much liquor, or not enough sleep. Or the combination. Not young anymore, Novak. Can't drink like a horse and kick like a mule much longer.

He stopped in front of Bikel's door, used the passkey and went in. Turning on the light he saw that Bikel's bag was packed. The bed was smooth. Nothing in the closet. Or in the bathroom medicine cabinet. Seals on all the glasses. Turning off the light he let himself out and locked the door. He thought, I wonder how far you'll get tonight, Eddie. Then he moved a few doors down the corridor and pressed the button.

It took a long while for her to come to the door and

when she did she looked older than he had ever seen her. Even in the dimness of the room her face was pale. A depression on the sofa showed where she had been sitting, staring out of the window at the vanishing light, watching night seep into the room.

One hand touched the hollow of her throat. "I didn't expect to see you."

"I have my rounds to make," he said, closing the door and walking further into the room. "Like the alley dog and the milkman."

Her laugh was artificial. "I didn't know the Tilden provided such personal service."

Novak sat down and stared up at her. "Relax, Julia," he said. "We've done business together. Before I went home I thought I'd make sure you were satisfied."

She placed one palm on the table, eased part of her weight onto it. The arm looked as sturdy as a piano leg. "Why...of course I'm satisfied."

"With the jewelry."

"Of course," she snapped. "Why shouldn't I be?" Her eyes narrowed. "However, since this morning I've thought things over, and I'm not at all sure my signing that receipt was a good idea."

Novak said nothing.

Julia Boyd cleared her throat. "I said I don't think I was wise to sign that receipt of yours. I was half-asleep, or I'm sure I wouldn't have."

Novak placed his fingertips together and shrugged. "Seemed routine to me. If an insurance company had recovered the jewelry you'd have had to sign a receipt." He squinted up at her. "It was a business transaction,

Julia. Jewelry and money changed hands. A receipt was in order."

Her tongue flicked out, moistened her lips quickly and disappeared.

Novak said, "What was it you had in mind?"

Nervously she said, "I'd like to have it back."

Novak looked down at his hands. "I need it, Mrs. Boyd."

"*Why* do you need it?"

"To protect myself."

She laughed shortly. "From what? Not me, surely?"

His hands spread. "From anything. In case any question should ever arise regarding the disappearance of the jewels and the circumstances surrounding their return." One of her hands was worrying a pleat in her skirt. He said, "Suppose someone got the idea I wasn't entirely honest—that I'd stolen the jewelry myself and sold it back to you. It might be a hard thing to make a case against me, but on the other hand, without your receipt I'd have a hell of a time disproving it." His head moved to one side. "See what I mean? Through you I had early knowledge that the jewels were in the hotel. It could be claimed that I decided to steal them and killed your husband in the process." He shook his head slowly. "Sorry, Mrs. Boyd. What you ask isn't possible." He stood up and moved past her.

"I'll pay you a thousand dollars for it," she said quickly.

He halted and stared at her. "It's worth that much to me."

"*How much?*" she yelled.

"Nothing," he said. "Nothing you could give me. You've got your jewelry, and I've got the receipt. That ends the transaction. Sorry I can't oblige."

"You son of a bitch," she snarled.

A crooked grin twisted his mouth. "Yeah, I'm a son of a bitch. I was useful last night when I took that dark walk down the country lane, but I'm a son of a bitch now. Think I don't know what made the difference?" He walked past her and put his hand on the doorknob. Glancing back he saw her rigid as a pillar of salt. He said, "Bikel ever tell you he was married, Julia? Well, that's no problem anymore. He's a widower now."

A long sigh escaped her lips. One hand was working in the folds of flesh around her throat.

"A pitiful little woman," he said leadenly. "Pathetic as a frozen sparrow, lying on a cheap bed in a cheap flophouse in a cheap part of town. Not everyone gets to die in the Tilden, Mrs. Boyd. Little people die where they can. When Eddie comes by, ask him what went through his mind when he walked in on her this morning. I'd like to hear it myself—whether he felt a twinge of remorse over what he's done or whether the only feeling was relief." His hand opened the door. Julia Boyd had not moved. Novak said, "Yesterday she went to a chapel because that was the only place she could go. By this morning she wasn't human any longer. Just something for the refuse heap." He went through the opening and pulled the door shut. Leaning against it he wiped his face slowly. His throat was tight, constricted. He swallowed hard and walked down the corridor.

Whatever Julia Boyd had been thinking before, she had other things to think about now. None of them very pleasant. He stabbed the elevator button and rode down to the lobby.

There was a stir of activity at the reception desk, guests checking in, bellhops scurrying off with baggage, snap of the bell captain's fingers. The revolving door turning steadily, swallowing, disgorging people. A place to spend the night. A room at the inn.

The reception clerk caught sight of him and motioned him over. From under the counter he pulled a folded telephone message, slipped it to Novak and went back to explaining something to an irritated lady.

Novak moved away and unfolded the message. Four words only: *No strain. Pike Hammond.*

Novak balled the message and dropped it in an ash stand. Nice of him to remember me, he thought, and straightened his lapels. That meant Hammond had picked up Barada's trail. But he still had to squeeze sixty-five grand out of him. Novak tried to think of the many ways a man like Pike Hammond could press juice out of a dry stone.

Andy the bell captain came up to him. "Nothing yet, Pete. You staying around a while?"

"Yeah. I'll gobble the coffee shop special before I go home."

He went over to the newsstand, bought an evening paper and carried it into the coffee shop. The cashier girl nodded to him as he mounted a stool at the counter. A waitress with an ivory smile took his order and asked if he wanted cream in his coffee.

Novak folded his paper, propped it against the sugar shaker and began reading baseball news. Not much action yet, too early in the season. Trades and deals and practice games in southern training camps. A game called for hail in Sarasota. Options, a sensational new southpaw from East Texas State. The waitress brought his dinner and Novak put the paper aside.

There was nothing wrong with the food. It was standard hotel coffee shop food with the usual decorative sprigs of defrosted parsley, but he hadn't much appetite. He toyed with the pork tenderloin, the frozen peas and string potatoes and began drinking his coffee. Like Julia Boyd, he had too many things on his mind. Plus a date at eight. Sylvia Riordan. She would have a pelt like wet sable and skin like waxed marble. Oh, yes, a fifth of bonded bourbon. Something to get at the corner store on his way home.

He was stirring his coffee moodily when a bellhop came up to him. "Phone call, Mr. Novak. Operator Three."

Novak nodded, glanced down at his hardly touched plate, signed the check, left a quarter for the waitress and went out to the ledge that held the house phones.

When the operator had switched his call he heard a voice crackle through the receiver. A voice as thin as a knife. "Novak?"

"Yeah."

"No names, understand? We met the other night in a certain lady's room."

"Get specific. I'm forever running into guys in dames' rooms. Part of the business."

"Save it for a sister act," the voice sneered. "The lady checked out today. Only she didn't get very far. She's here right now. She wants to see you, Novak. She can barely stand the pain, Get it?"

His flesh was clammy with sweat. Chilled fingers gripped the black rubber handle. "Let me talk to her," he said unsteadily.

"Sure. I'm taking the phone to her."

A moment of silence, then Paula's voice, strained and breathy. "Pete...*don't*—" then the hard crack of a slap and a scream, fading as the phone was jerked away.

The voice was cold and vicious. "She's not herself tonight, Novak. A great little kidder. She meant to say she wants you to come and straighten a few things out. Any objections?"

"No," Novak said in a cracked voice.

A snotty chuckle. "The sooner you get here the sooner she can relax. And stash the heater home. Understand?"

"I understand."

"You got ten minutes to get to the corner of Vermont and Fourteenth. South side. Any cops and the lady gets hurt." The line clicked off, and Novak lowered the receiver. Stiffly his fingers released it on the cradle. His eyes traveled to his wristwatch and marked the time. He could make it in five minutes if he hurried.

Novak spun around, jogged to his office. He flipped on the lights and spun the safe dial. He missed it the first time, swore and forced unsteady fingers to retrace the combination. This time the drawer opened, and he pulled out Paula's chrome-plated automatic. He jacked a shell into the chamber, clicked off the safety and bent over. Pulling up his right trouser leg he lowered his garter, tightened it and slid the automatic down against the back of his leg below the bulge of the calf. The garter would hold it in place until he needed it.

Jerking off his coat he shed the shoulder holster and jammed the .38 in his inside pocket. Then he opened a desk drawer and took out a bone-handled folding knife. The knife he dropped in his right coat pocket. Then he snatched his hat from the rack and raced out of the office.

On K Street he dodged through ebbing sidewalk crowds, pulse throbbing in his temples, throat tight and raw. It was cool enough for gloves and a topcoat but there was sweat around his neck and his palms were damp, fingers stiff.

Past the Investment Building, then only a short block to Vermont. Traffic swarmed past, tires snicking like knives in green wood. A blur of neon signs, the lighted window of a drugstore jammed with cheap toys and plastic skeleton models. Straining he peered through the darkness and saw the lighted statue at Thomas Circle. Below it a steady whirl of cars rounding the circle, cutting off, converging within the close-packed maze. His lips were dry. He moistened them, glanced at his watch. Two minutes to go. They had planned it neatly.

Past the Burlington Hotel. Now he could see the point where Fourteenth cut across Vermont. The spot where he was supposed to wait. Inside his coat the re-

volver banged loosely against his ribs. His hip sockets
ached. He sucked cold air into his lungs, coughed and
kept going. Dimmed headlights of circling cars stared
like unseeing eyes. Novak reached the point and rested
against the lamppost. Breathing deeply, he saw that
there was a minute to go.

Slowly the pounding in his temples eased and his
pulse slowed. His hatband was clammy. He took it off,
wiped it on his sleeve, fitted it on his head again.

His eyes searched each car that followed the outside lane. Beige, blue, dandelion yellow; new, old,
dented fenders, paint spots on the doors. All anonymous. No way to tell which was the contact car.
Glancing down he saw hands clenched into hard fists.
He straightened the fingers, flexed the stiff joints and
rubbed the palms against his legs. His left foot toed
the back of his right leg. The pistol was still in place.
Paula's garter gun.

Squinting at the traveling wheel of cars he saw one
cross to the outside lane and head for the lamppost.
The driver stuck out his hand, slowed and stopped
beside Novak. A dark blue Chevy sedan.

From the rear seat a voice barked, "We ain't got a
world of time."

Blocked cars honked their horns. Novak stepped off
the curb, yanked the door open and got in. The car
jerked forward, slamming him against the seat. A voice
rumbled, "You're covered, Novak. Lift the arms."

Novak raised his arms, felt a hand patting his pockets,
his chest. It prodded the revolver, dipped into his coat
and pulled it out.

"Naughty boy," the voice chided. "You was told not to bring the iron."

Novak grunted, lowered his arms, fitted himself into the seat corner.

The man who had taken his revolver stowed it in a coat pocket and leered at him. "That gives me two. And none for you. Like it?"

"Not much," Novak croaked and saw the man's head turn.

"Okay, Tags. We ain't followed. Feed it some gas. Ben's waiting."

The car had made a half circle and come onto Vermont Avenue again. It headed north, picking up speed.

16

Novak's hands gripped his knees. His face looked de-
jected, defeated. His eyes studied the other man. Hatless and hair too long. The eyes were narrow and his
forehead was too thin. One of the guys who had played
soccer with him in the alley.

Novak leaned forward, said softly. "How's the nose
coming along, Tags?"

The driver snarled. *"You son of a bitch!"*

Novak leaned back and grinned in the darkness.
"Someone ought to invent a new word. That's all I get
called these days."

Beside him the other man grunted nastily. "Be grateful you lasted so long, pal."

Novak nodded soberly. "I ought to be at that. Only
last night you had me in the headlights, an easy target.
This pickup looks like afterthought."

"Never mind, pal. You'll find out soon enough. You
ain't getting this ride so's you can jawbone us helpless.
Keep the mouth shut. Get it?"

"Suits me. The bad grammar gets boring anyway."

A hand cuffed the side of his face. Novak rubbed
the spot tenderly. The guy spat, "That's only the beginning. Keep the lip zipped."

Novak gripped his knees harder, felt the car lurch

to the right and saw a street sign flash past. *Melrose St.*
They must not care that he saw the route they were
taking. That could mean he wouldn't be making the
trip again. They could be right. Shivering, he wrapped
his arms together for warmth.

A slewing turn to the left, half a block more and the
car bumped over a curb driveway and slowed to a stop
beside the back door of a dark house.

Tags turned off the engine, got out. He poked his
face in the rear window. "Let's move, Al."

"Cover him," Al said, opened the door and got out.
He held the door opened and drawled, "Last mile."

Novak's teeth bared, he shifted along the seat and
stepped down, hands lifted to protect his head against
a whistling sap.

It was an old frame house with a screened back
porch. He followed Tags up four wooden steps, through
a creaking screen door and waited. Al jabbed a gun in
his ribs. "Slow and easy," he breathed. "Nothing fast,
pal. Just follow the man."

Through a crack in the door shade Novak could see
a glimmer of light. Tags turned a key in the rusty lock
and pushed ahead. A kitchen with a linoleum floor. No
smell of recent cooking.

A dark narrow hallway. The heavy clump of their
feet on the dusty floor.

Tags elbowed the door open and Novak followed
him into the living room. The shades were down and
the light came from two wooden floor lamps. A fringed
imitation oriental carpet, worn smooth in patches.
Rockers with stained petit-point seats, a low stuffed

sofa, a round writing table and a couple of Windsor chairs in bad repair.

Ben Barada sat on the sofa staring up at Novak. He wore a yellow silk shirt, cuffs rolled back and no tie. His face looked hard and desperate. The girl was tied in one of the chairs, hands behind the chairback, cords around her ankles. Even in the amber light angry patches stood out on her face. Her hair was disarrayed and the torn linen blouse showed one bare shoulder, marked with deep finger bruises. Her lips were puffed and her cheeks showed traces of dried salt. Her eyes prayed to Novak.

Barada smiled thinly, blew smoke at Novak and said, "At last everyone's together. Glad you came, Novak?"

Al said, "He tried to sneak a rod, Ben."

"He would." Eyes flickered back to Novak. "Everyone together," he repeated. "You, my faithful ex-wife and me." He got up slowly and walked to Novak. "Funny what a dame sees in a guy. Paula says you're okay. To me you're just another dumb sucker. Anything to say, cheapy?"

"Hello, jailbird."

Barada's face convulsed. His right hand stabbed out, slamming Novak's belly. Novak doubled over. Nausea flared through his mouth. He retched, staggered to one side and straightened painfully. Barada was stroking the knuckles of his right hand. "Thought you were tough," he sneered.

The words echoed through the silent room. Novak rolled his shoulders and glanced down at Paula. His face was thin and bitter. He licked his lips and felt his hands clench. "Sorry," he muttered.

"Don't blame yourself," she said huskily. "It's my fault. All of it."

"How true, baby," Barada jeered. "Starting with you and Boyd. Got lonely at night, didn't it? So lonely you had to share your bed." His lips drew back over his teeth. "What about me in Joliet? Ever bother to give your husband a thought?"

"We've gone over that," she said wearily. "Tell Novak what you want. The sight of you makes me want to vomit."

A guffaw from Al in the corner. Barada whirled around. "Enough outa you," he snarled. "Toss me the car keys."

Tags spoke. "They're in the car, Ben."

"Move."

Novak could hear Tags cross behind him, walk down the passageway into the kitchen. Barada turned to him. "Okay, sucker, Paula spilled what you did for her the other night—how you moved the body back to Boyd's room. Just one of those helpful guys. Or was there maybe a payoff somewhere?" His eyes turned to Paula. "Did you get so grateful you slipped Novak the jewels?"

"Someone took them," she said dully. "Novak was with me when I found they were gone."

Barada laughed shortly. "They were gone all right because I took them. I was down in the lobby when I saw you go out. I skipped back to your room, found

Boyd's body on the bed and shook down the place."
He moved his head slowly. "I found jewelry and skipped
out with it. What a surprise," he said thinly. "Muzzlers.
A phony set."

"The stuff you sold back last night for a grand,"
Novak said.

"Sure. I figured Paula still had the others, but she
claims not. She's not the bravest little roundheels in the
world and the more fists she eats the more she claims
she only had one set. That makes Boyd a cheapskate—
which I doubt—or maybe someone else has them." His
eyes drilled into Novak. "Know what I think, peeper? I
think you latched onto the real ones somewhere along
the line and figured on giving the insurance company
a little play—after we'd all left town."

Novak blinked at Barada. "The phonies you took—
where were they?"

Barada snorted. "Under her pillow begging to be
found."

Novak saw Paula's eyebrows draw together. Her
mouth opened, but he warned her with his eyes. To
Barada he said, "I returned the phony set to Julia Boyd.
Having done that how the hell could I try to make a
deal with the insurance company for the real ones—if
I had them?"

Barada shrugged. "Everyone makes mistakes," he
said coldly. "I make them, Paula's made some, and so
have you. But this is the time we straighten things
out."

The porch door slammed as Tags went out to the
driveway.

Novak's palms were sweaty. His throat felt like cold wax.

Barada said, "The jewels, Novak. You got them, I want them."

"In exchange for what?"

Barada shrugged. "You walk out the door—the dame too, if you want her."

"Doesn't sound like much of a trade," Novak husked. "Suppose I don't go along with it?"

Barada's face went murderous. "This is an old empty house, Novak. Nobody comes around much. Not even the milkman. Maybe in a month or so a cop might peep in the window. Know what he'd find?"

Novak's mouth tasted like dry sand.

Barada's voice rose. "He'd find two bodies here. You and the dame. A pistol between you—yours. A suicide pact." One hand rolled down a yellow cuff, buttoned it. "That's what he'd find."

Paula's throat made a gasp of horror.

Novak blinked at him. "I wouldn't care for that," he said hoarsely. "Not at all." His shoulders slumped, hands opened and closed emptily. Then his eyes narrowed. "How do I know you'll let us go?"

Barada's eyes flickered. He buttoned the other cuff. "That's the chance you take."

Novak turned to Paula. "Long odds, gray-eyes," he said huskily. "It's up to you."

"No one's asking her," Barada flared.

"I'm asking her," Novak snarled.

Paula writhed in the chair, straining her wrists and ankles against the cords that bound them. Her lips parted and she moaned, "He'll kill us. Don't do it!"

Barada leaped toward the chair. His hand snaked back and the palm slashed across her face. Her head snapped to one side, and she screamed in pain.

Novak jerked around. Al was against the wall with a gun in his hand. "Easy," he spat.

Barada's eyes were wild. His arms shook. Novak went slowly to the writing table and sat down. From Paula's chair came the sound of racking sobs. A soul in torment, utterly without hope.

A sheet of paper lay on the table. Novak reached for his pen. He wondered what was keeping Tags so long. Uncapping the pen he wrote the date at the top of the sheet and turned around. "They're in my desk," he said thickly. "I'll write a note to the night clerk. He'll get the envelope and turn it over."

On Barada's face was a deadly look. He must be mad, Novak thought. A hophead or stir-crazy. He said, "Paula didn't kill Boyd. Someone else did. Someone who waited there for Boyd to show up with the ninety-grand payoff money. Your story's a little thin, Barada. Maybe you were the guy. The cops would sort of like that idea."

"You're wasting time," Barada snapped. "Start writing."

Novak gave him a crooked grin. "Time's running out, but not for me. The clock's turning, minutes are fading but I've got plenty of time. You forced Paula into trying to get money from Boyd in return for the jewels. Why? Because you owed sixty-five grand to Pike Hammond. Well, Hammond's in town. Making you the guy in the big hurry, not me."

Barada's face was frozen. "Pike?" he gasped. "You're lying."

Novak's head moved slowly. "How would I know if I hadn't talked to him?"

On the porch the screen door slammed. Tags with the car keys. Careful boys, worrying over car thieves. The thought made him smile grimly. He laid the pen on the table and looked up at Barada. "My mother was Irish," he said quietly, "and Celts have the gift of second sight." His head tilted back. "I look at you, Barada, and I see a skull. A bleached skull with hollow eye sockets and a hole in place of a nose. Even as far away as you are you stink of death. It's perched on your shoulder licking its filthy lips and waiting." He laughed roughly. "You can't frighten me, Barada. You're as good as dead." His elbow struck the pen, rolling it under the table. As he bent down for it he heard footsteps along the hallway. His hand groped, slid up his trouser cuff, grabbed the pistol and snatched it free. Whirling he dropped to his knees and shot Al. Twice. The reports were sharp and clear. Al bellowed in agony and slid to the floor.

Novak got up, backed to the wall and saw Al's body shudder and lie still. His gaze fastened on Barada. "Everyone's been so damn clever the little things get overlooked. Like this." He moved the snout of the chrome-plated automatic. "On your knees, Barada. Untie her. Fast."

His eyes gazed at the dark doorway. By now Tags should be among them. What had stopped him? From the corner of his eye he saw Barada fumbling at Paula's ankles, then a lightning movement of one hand.

Before he could move there was a gun in Barada's hand. A small one with twin barrels. A gambler's gun, he thought as he dropped sideways and heard it bark. Then another shot. Deafening and from the doorway.

Barada made no sound. A little derringer fell from one hand. The other was already covering a stain spreading across his chest. The face grimaced horribly, the eyes went glassy and vacant. Suddenly he pitched forward.

From the floor Novak scanned the man in the doorway. A man in a houndstooth jacket and a brittle smile on his handsome face. The cool eyes fixed on Novak.

Pike Hammond said, "You didn't know about Ben's derringer. I did." He opened his coat, put away the Colt. Then he stepped into the room and stared down at Barada. "The most expensive shot I ever made," he said thickly. "Sixty-five grand it cost me."

"You can afford it."

Hammond's eyes darted quickly at him. "What would you know about that?"

"You don't work for anyone, Pike. Most everyone works for you. That's the word from St. Louis."

Hammond shrugged, lifted his left foot and toed Barada's body as if it were garbage. "So long, welsher," he said tautly. "See you in the hot place."

Paula had fainted. Novak untied the cords, carried her to the sofa, laid her gently down. When he looked around Hammond was bending over touching Al's jugular vein. He shook his head slowly. "Fair shooting,

Novak. Even if it took two." He straightened up and went to the sofa. For a long time he studied Paula's face and then he turned to Novak. Almost reverently he said, "I never saw her before, just heard about her. She's as lovely as they said. Maybe she won't like my killing Big Ben."

"She could get over it," Novak said in a strained voice. "Take her on a long trip, Pike."

His lips pursed. "I could ask her," he said in a distant voice. Then one eyebrow lifted. "Unless you staked out a claim?"

Novak swallowed. "I couldn't keep her in perfume," he said dully, turned and searched for the two ejected shells until he found them. By then Paula's eyes were open. She was staring up at Pike Hammond who was seated beside her. Novak heard her say, "I don't know you."

Novak dropped the empty shells in his pocket, blew into the pistol barrel. "Meet Pike Hammond from St. Louis. Owner and proprietor of the Stallion Club. The guy who banks what the suckers lose."

Hammond pulled off his tweed hat. "Pleased to meet you, Miss Norton," he said gravely. "We ought not stay around here too long."

Novak said, "What happened to the guy who was supposed to come through the doorway?"

Hammond turned slightly, and a smile played over his lips. "He faded early. How long he'll sleep is anyone's guess."

Paula extended one arm, and Hammond helped her

sit upright. She closed her eyes, swayed and opened her eyes again. "I had some bags," she said quietly. "In the other room, I think."

Hammond nodded. One hand went inside his coat pocket, pulled out the ostrich wallet and the gloved thumb riffled a deck of crisp bills. Nothing under a hundred. He said, "You've earned something. Name it."

Novak's mouth twisted. "You shot Barada, not me. I ought to be paying you."

"I mean it," Hammond said levelly.

"So do I. Anyway, it's crook money."

Hammond's face darkened. The wallet disappeared inside his coat. His dark eyes held Novak's. Hammond said, "We'll let that one pass. Money's money. It has no race, sex or politics. Money isn't right or wrong. Not by itself. For a peeper you've got too damn much pride."

"That's why I stay a peeper."

Hammond turned and spoke to Paula. "My car's a couple of blocks away. Shall we get going?"

Her eyes were larger than he had ever seen them before. She walked to Novak and laid her arms on his shoulders. Her fingers laced behind his neck. "Just like that," she said bitterly, "you'd let me walk away."

His stomach was achingly hollow, his arms leaden as he drew her against him. "I've got a walk-up flat," he said in a voice that wavered, "a TV set and an electric toaster. Sometimes there's hot water and sometimes not. I keep long hours, and when I get back to the flat I'm usually too tired to do more than mix a drink and stagger off to bed. That's no life for you, beautiful. It's no life for anyone." He bent his head and caressed the bruised lips gently. "Thanks for thinking of me, beautiful. Buy me a drink next time you breeze through town."

"I'll have money," she whispered. "Half of Chalmers' fortune."

He shook his head slowly. "After you told me about the call I checked the switchboard operators. No long-distance calls had gone to your room. It was a fake. Tags or Al impersonated the lawyer. To get you out of the hotel. Sorry, beautiful."

Her head drew back, her face was dazed. Her eyes stared at him unbelievingly.

Hammond cleared his throat. "Let's shove off. No telling who heard the shooting." He picked up Paula's bags.

The gray eyes had misted. Novak drew her arms apart and kissed the side of one cheek. Shakily she turned and began pulling on her coat.

Hammond said, "Need my gun for a prop?"

"Registered?"

Hammond nodded.

"No good then. I'll set enough of a scene to satisfy cops who don't get feverish over hood killings."

"Any time you get to St. Louis, look me up," Hammond said as he moved past Novak. "The Stallion Club. Ask any cabbie."

"Sure. You'll stand me a drink. We'll have a cigarette and chat for half an hour trying to remember what the hell it was all about." He lifted his hat, ran one hand through his hair and saw Paula turn and breathe a kiss. Her cheeks were moist. The amber light plated them with burnished gold.

He heard their footsteps going along the passageway to the kitchen. The screen door opened, closed softly, and then there was silence.

Novak got out a cigarette with unsteady fingers, lighted it and heard a cracked voice saying, "Take good care of her, Pike." He felt terribly alone. He drew one hand across the side of his face, shook himself and went over beside the writing table. He gathered his pen from the floor, crumpled the sheet of paper he had written on and shoved it in his pocket. His eyes searched the wall until he found the hole drilled by Barada's derringer. A small hole, .22 maybe. And a close miss. The derringer was for under-the-table work, not a gunfight. Barada had learned the lesson too late.

Novak took the two empty shells from his pocket, wiped them and dropped them near Barada's body. There was a big red hole staining the back of Barada's yellow shirt. Colt .45. Nice shooting, Pike.

He wiped the chrome-plated pistol and laid it in Barada's upturned palm. He pressed the slack fingers around it, remembering to touch the index to the trigger, and then he placed the pistol a foot from Barada's hand and picked up the derringer. Carrying it over to Al's body he wiped it and repeated the process, leaving the little gun a yard from Al's arm. One of his shots had torn through Al's jaw. The other had entered the throat. There was no exit hole.

His lips were as dry as brick. Moistening them he flicked ash from the cigarette and stared around the room. Nothing else to do. The setting wouldn't fool a moron.

In the distance he heard a car engine start. The car backed, turned and ground away. As he listened his throat tightened again. He swallowed hard, turned and went through the passageway into the kitchen. Covering the doorknob with his handkerchief he pulled it open, closed it and walked down the steps.

He almost stumbled over Tags' body beside the car. There was a steady heartbeat and muffled sounds came from the gauze-stuffed snout. Novak opened the car door, slid across the seat and found the ignition keys.

Without turning on the lights he started the engine and backed the car out of the driveway.

17

The moon was a tuft of dirty cotton, clouds rafted the starless sky, the air had the heavy taste of rain.

As he drove he tried not to think about the last half hour on Melrose Street but his nostrils still held the bitter scent of gunsmoke. The cigarette tasted like smoldering straw but it was better than the reek of cordite. In his mind he saw two dead bodies lying on the floor of a dusty room; but for a little luck they would have been his and Paula's. He thought of Morely and wondered if Bikel had returned to the Tilden. He thought of a wasted little woman on a chipped iron bed. He thought of a fat woman in an expensive suite, staring at the ragged moon and waiting.

His body was spent, his mind numb. He found his head nodding, attention drifting from the road. For a while he fought fatigue, and then he stopped at a diner and gulped two cups of black coffee. When he crawled behind the wheel again he knew he could last another couple of hours.

Movie houses were disgorging people from the early show. Taverns were doing a normal Thursday night business. Shopping center lots were jammed with cars. He wondered whose car he was driving. Not a rental car, probably stolen. Time to start it on the way back to its owner.

At Q Street he turned and drove down Kingman Place to a dark curb under a low tree. He cut the motor, dropped the keys on the floor and got out. Wiping his prints from the door handle he jogged back to Vermont and waited until a cruising cab pulled over.

In front of the Tilden, the doorman opened the cab door and beckoned to a waiting couple. When he saw Novak paying the driver he said, "They're looking for you inside, Pete. Andy says its important."

Novak nodded, hurried into the lobby. The bell captain was standing near the reception counter, fingers drumming against his leg. When he saw Novak he hurried over. "Jeez, Pete, where you been?" he complained. "Lieutenant Morely wants you to call him right away."

"Bikel ever get back?"

Andy shook his head. "If he did no one saw him—and I ain't hardly took my eyes off the elevators."

"Thanks, Andy." Novak strode to the desk phone, asked the operator for Police Headquarters and got Morely on the phone in less than a minute. Morely said, "Well, pal, we bagged the medicine man."

"Where?"

"Mortuary."

"Dead?"

Morely chuckled dryly. "Naw, he's feeling pretty sick but he's still among the living. We picked him up trying to claim his wife's body for burial."

"The sentimental type. What are you holding him on?"

"Violating drug control laws, for one thing. Material

witness in the death of his wife for another. And if that ain't enough we can toss in Boyd's death. I figure Dr. Edward Bikel will be with us quite a little while."

"Mrs. Boyd know?"

"Not from me."

"He gets to make a phone call, you know."

"He ain't asked yet. When he does, maybe he won't have the necessary dime."

"Mind if I tell Mrs. Boyd?"

Morely grunted. "Help yourself. She can't run a shyster down here before morning and by then we'll have wrung considerable sweat out of our doctor." There was a thoughtful pause. "Bikel had quite a bit to gain from Boyd's death. How do you like it he gunned Boyd so's he could marry the widow?"

"And left the body in the widow's room? Sounds sort of scatterbrained."

"The doc's on the feeble side. Maybe he used up all his strength pulling the trigger and couldn't budge the corpse. Anyway, we're asking him. By morning we may have something for the papers."

"You may at that," Novak said, "but I seem to remember your liking Barada as Boyd's murderer. What happened to that?"

"Motive," Morely said irritably. "A guy like Barada don't kill just because some john's shacked up with his wife. Blackmail, yes, because it's profitable. How could he get a nickel out of murdering Boyd?"

"Maybe he got the jewels."

"You fixed that one, pal," Morely said bitterly. "I

might believe it like I believe in the True Cross, but Mrs. Boyd has the jewels now."

"He got a grand out of them," Novak said evenly.

"Canary feed. Hell, he coulda realized half their insured value from the insurance company. If he killed Boyd for the jewels why didn't he make them pay off?"

"There's an answer to that," Novak murmured. "You figure it out." Then he cut the connection, massaged his closed eyes and crossed the lobby to an open elevator.

Riding to the fifth, Novak slumped wearily in the corner, opening and closing his hands. His belly ached where the muscles had bunched from Barada's low punch. If he let himself concentrate on it he could probably get sick again. If he tried.

The doors slid apart, and Novak stepped into the fifth floor hall. Walking to Bikel's room he keyed the door and went inside. He turned on the lights and stared around. Bikel's bag was still there, packed and waiting for the absent owner. Might as well check him out and free the room. Novak hooked onto the bag, carried it out to the corridor and locked the door. Then he walked further down the hall. As far as Suite 515. Thirty-five skins a day, plus District Tax. Now single occupancy. The widow of the late Chalmers Boyd. Novak pressed the door button and waited.

Far down the corridor a door opened and shut. Low voices threaded through the heavy air. From inside 515 no sound.

Novak pressed the button again. Longer this time.

It made a thin muffled sound. Like a dog whining in a cellar.

Pressing his ear to the door panel he listened, got out the master key and opened the door.

In the sitting room a single lamp cast a subdued glow against the naked wall. Enough to show a woman sitting on the sofa, face turned toward the dark window. As he closed the door the click of the lock seemed to rouse her. The eyes turned toward him, and he saw the pudgy doll-face, the heavy arms, the mountainous bosom. One hand covered something on the cushion beside her thigh. The light was too indistinct to show him what it was.

As Novak walked toward her, dull eyes regarded him unblinkingly.

He lowered the bag, chose a chair not far from the sofa and settled into it heavily. Pulling off his hat he tossed it onto the table. Moistening his cracked lips he said, "Full circle, Julia."

Her mouth opened and closed. The lips formed no words.

"Back where it all started," he said in a thick voice. "Barada's dead—along with the hood who called about your jewelry. I thought you'd be interested to know."

"You killed them?"

"Barada was shot by Pike Hammond—a gambler Barada owed sixty-five thousand dollars to. Hammond's from St. Louis. Possibly you've heard of him."

Her head moved. Yes.

"I killed the other. He took one gun from me, forgot to look for another. The mistake was fatal."

She said, "You are an evil man. A wicked man. You disrupt peoples' lives. You kill without compassion."

Novak laughed dryly. "They would have killed me, Mrs. Boyd. Entirely without pity. And the girl as well."

Her body moved forward slightly. "The slut—where is she?"

"Safe, Mrs. Boyd. And far from here."

"She wronged me," the voice said vacantly. "She wronged me grievously."

"Your husband wronged you. And long before he met Paula Norton."

Her head nodded pensively. The fingers of her left hand twitched. The lips said, "I was a young girl once. I had a normal body. There were many who thought of me as beautiful. Then I became unhappy. My body grew until it became this bloated thing." Her tone filled with disgust. "Chalmers was to blame. It was his fault that I became the ugliness I am."

"He's paid for it," Novak observed. "The account's settled. And you have your jewelry. You must have wanted it badly."

Her head moved negatively, her body shifted slightly. From the city beyond the window drifted the low purr of night traffic in the streets, the whistle of the night steamer to Old Point Comfort.

Julia Boyd said, "He gave it to me on our twenty-fifth anniversary. I wore it once and put it away. It made me look even more grotesque. I hated it. Then he gave it to the woman he admired. He thought I didn't know, but I did. I found out, and I challenged him, insisted he get it back."

"What else did you find out?"

Her shoulders moved disdainfully. "Chalmers was a coward. He was afraid to ask her for it. So he had copies made. He gave them to me. It was supposed to deceive me. But the detectives told me."

Novak nodded. "By then Paula had broken with him, making the return of the real jewelry even more difficult. Because her husband was out of prison and in need of money. He had lost sixty-five thousand dollars to Pike Hammond, probably as much to others. His luck had gone bad. To Barada your jewelry meant a stake, last chance to pull himself out of a narrow hole. I think Paula would have returned the jewelry when she found out it was yours—only Barada wouldn't let her. Maybe you learned that too."

"He was a desperate man," she said heavily. "His kind will do anything for money."

"Even murder," Novak said. "I learned that tonight." He sucked in a deep breath. The bedroom doorway was dark. From somewhere outside came the whine of a vacuum cleaner. A late check-out. Readying the room for anonymous guests. A transient place. A hotel never sleeps.

Novak said, "You thought by reporting the jewelry as stolen you could put more pressure on Paula for its return. But out of some sense of loyalty to Paula, Chalmers refused to make the report. Or he could have felt that paying for it was the easier way. When he came back here after talking to me you must have been furious with him. He was ready to pay Paula the sum Barada was asking. I was with her when he telephoned to arrange a meeting."

Her eyes narrowed. In the dim light they were without color, without depth. Holes in a white mask. She said, "It was *my* money. Everything that Chalmers owned belonged to me."

"Not an ideal arrangement," Novak said dryly. "No man would like that kind of arrangement for long."

"He had no choice," she said scornfully. "Without me he was nothing. A shirt-sleeved bookkeeper in my father's bank. That was how Chalmers started. It was what he would have had to go back to if I threw him out."

"Lovely people," Novak muttered. "Pillars of suburban society."

Julia Boyd touched one finger to the corner of her mouth, lowered her hand absently. Novak said, "I heard Paula refuse to meet Chalmers the night he was killed. Her ex-husband had given her a beating and shown her what he really was—a vicious hoodlum. She was shocked, confused; she wanted time to think. So she told your husband she would talk to him the next morning, then went out for a long walk. But by next morning your husband was dead, and Paula was under suspicion. Only she didn't kill him." He stared at the white face. "The body was found here, Mrs. Boyd, not in Paula's room where it was supposed to be found. That was the second thing that went wrong."

A frayed sigh came from her lips. Novak's throat grated like emery paper. He swallowed, said, "We haven't discussed Dr. Bikel yet. The ubiquitous medicine man and herb specialist. The guy who brews mescaline and vends it in his little shop. The guy who gave you the sympathy and understanding you never got from your husband."

Her eyes moved. She looked slowly at her hands, then stared at a point on the wall over Novak's shoulder.

"The police have Eddie. They wanted to talk to him, Mrs. Boyd. About the way his wife died. Did she kill herself, or did he recommend an overdose of something to calm her nerves? Bikel was a small-timer, Mrs. Boyd. An old chiseler settled down in an ostensibly respectable business. Married and leading a shabby life where pennies counted. Then somehow he hooked onto you. I see him studying your case and seeing in it a chance to be big-time and legitimate. His last chance. It wouldn't take much intuition to guess the relationship between you and Chalmers. Or you may have told him about Paula and your husband. That could have encouraged his idea of marrying you eventually. But of course he was already married.

"His wife must have known his plans. I can see him talking over the future with her matter-of-factly, pleading for a quiet divorce and promising to provide for her afterward. Even handsomely. But when he planned this trip with you I can see her getting desperate, threatening to destroy his scheme by revealing to you that Bikel had a wife. In any case, the day he checked in here he sent a telegram. It told her not to come to Washington and promised he'd arrange things to her satisfaction. But she came anyway. Yesterday afternoon in Bikel's room they had a nasty scene, and she ran out crying. From there she scurried to the chapel. To pray, Mrs. Boyd. In your set prayer isn't overly fashionable, I imagine. Prayer from the heart, anyway. And this morning she was dead. A shabby, wizened little creature. Bikel's wife and helpmate. No one to trot around in moneyed circles. Just an embarrassment to the doctor." His hands curved stiffly over his knees. "But she's dead now, and Bikel's free. Do I get an invitation to the wedding?"

Julia Boyd said nothing. Her mouth grimaced, her tongue licked her lips slowly.

Novak said, "I brought his bag here. The doctor won't need it for a while. He's spending the night at Police Headquarters, Mrs. Boyd. No need to wait for him any longer."

Her head lowered. The heavy shoulders came forward, and her body shivered. "He deceived me," she whimpered. "Pretending to love me when he was married. Men have always tricked me. Like Chalmers." Her throat sucked breath stridently, and her eyes lifted. "When Chalmers married me I was an innocent girl. I believed he loved me, but he was false. He only wanted my money—like Bikel." Her eyes dropped away, and her voice hollowed. "All I ever wanted was love and happiness. And this is what I became."

For a brief moment he felt a surge of pity for her; then he remembered the house on Melrose Street and his voice steeled. "It must have been a brutal shock to find out your husband had tried to palm fake jewelry on you—another in a series of bitter disillusionments with your husband. But you kept them and the time came when they were useful."

Her eyes had brightened. Her head slanted to one side as she listened. Novak said, "Somehow you managed to get Chalmers into Paula's room while she was out. You shot him in the bedroom, recovered the payoff money from his pocket and the real jewels from her makeup bag and planted the fakes under her pillow. Only minutes later Barada found them there and took them away. Bad luck for you. But by then you were back here and in bed."

"Someone moved Chalmers' body," she whined. "Was it you?"

He nodded. "How did you get into her room? Bribe the hall maid?"

A smile moved her lips. "I stood at the door and called the maid. She assumed it was my room and let me in. Then I called Chalmers by telephone, pretending I was the girl, and told him to come over. I left the door ajar and waited in the bedroom. You know the rest." A tremor racked her body. As though she were sitting in an icy draft. But the window was closed, the warm air still and heavy.

Novak said, "You couldn't tell the police that Paula had been given your jewels by Chalmers because your knowledge would have suggested to them that you might have taken violent means to get them back. So the fakes had to be found where you planted them. You didn't know Barada had taken them; so you hired me to discover them. Only my heart wasn't in the job. Yes, I sold out to her, if you want to put it that way, but not for financial considerations—because I didn't think she killed your husband. More bad luck for you. But things picked up when Barada's thug called and offered the jewels for sale. You knew they were phonies, but you couldn't admit it. So I became useful again—the perfect witness to the manner of their recovery. Only before I brought them to you I stopped at a jeweler's and had them examined. So knowing they were fakes I got you to sign a receipt acknowledging that I had returned legitimate jewelry to you. At the time I was surprised you let me get away with it, but later you must have seen the spot it put you in, and so you tried to buy back the receipt. I needed it to prove I had acted in good faith and at your request—in case you or anyone else got the idea I might have lifted the jewels myself and maneuvered their return."

He felt his shoulders sag. Fatigue was chilling him. He swallowed, blinked and went on. "Barada was pretty mad when he found he had only a set of muzzlers for all his trouble. He figured Paula still had the real ones and tried to beat them out of her. She didn't have them, of course, so Barada decided I might. He invited me to a deserted house and threatened me with death. A desperate man, Mrs. Boyd, to use your words, but not over-intelligent. He wasn't smart enough to reason that if neither Paula or I had the real jewels you must have them, and that you were willing to pay a grand to get the fakes in order to protect yourself. To you it was a small price in terms of your security. In time Barada might have realized that whoever had the real jewels probably had shot Chalmers Boyd, and then you would have been in for blackmail. But that doesn't matter now. How much did Bikel know?"

Listlessly she said, "He acted as though he knew I killed Chalmers, but he said nothing."

"Why should he? It suited him that your husband was dead. And of course his pose was an eligible suitor attracted by what you were, not by your money. Quite a blow to your pride when you learned he had a wife, though I doubt the way she died troubled you. So Bikel became another man who lied and deceived you. And you were waiting for him to return."

He got up slowly and went over to her. Emptily she said, "He should have told me in the beginning. I would have understood and helped."

"But he neglected to. And he destroyed what was left of your illusions." His arm reached down, but her hand lifted suddenly. It held a small blue steel automatic.

"Yes," she said hoarsely, "I've been waiting for him. But you'll do as well. Everything went wrong because of you. God, how I hate you Novak!"

"You're mad," he said thickly. "Put it away."

Her eyes flickered uncertainly. "Why should I?"

"Because I came here to give you a chance."

Her eyebrows furrowed and she blinked. "What kind of a chance?"

"Kill me and you'll burn in the chair. An unpleasant death, Mrs. Boyd. Ever see that photo of Winnie Ruth Judd fighting twenty thousand volts? It snaps the spine like matchwood, roasts the flesh. Even the teeth turn black." He stepped back slowly. "There are easier ways to die. There's the way Mrs. Bikel died. And there's the gun in your hand—the one you killed your husband with. That's the break I'm giving you."

The sound of the vacuum cleaner had stopped. The room was silent, the air stiflingly heavy.

As he watched, the hand lowered, the face turned away. He could feel sweat roll down his chest. When the pistol rested on the cushion once more he sucked a deep breath, turned and moved toward the door, legs heavy as timber.

When he had locked the door behind him he leaned back for a moment, resting against it, and then he began walking toward the elevator.

Wordlessly he rode down to the street level. His brain was numb, his throat chokingly tight as he crossed the lobby and went out the side door.

Clouds hid the moon. A thin mist drifted down dampening his face and hands. Long before morning it would thicken into a pelting rain. Along K Street the tires of moving cars made dull slapping sounds on the wet pavement. Turning up his collar Novak trudged along until he reached a lighted glass brick front. For a while he stared up at the sign over the doorway, and then he rang the night bell.

It took five minutes for Doc Robinson to open the door. His gray hair was rumpled, and he squinted at Novak through rimless glasses. "Come in," he said gruffly. "Don't stand there in the rain."

Novak moved into the lighted reception room and the veterinarian closed the door behind him. As he walked toward Novak he said, "Ever find the lady, Pete?"

Novak sat down on a leather-covered bench and wiped moisture from the brim of his hat. "I found her," he said. "Then I lost her again. Is the pup still here?"

Doc Robinson nodded. "They got you walking dogs now? I thought that was a bellhop chore."

"I do a little bit of everything," Novak said tiredly. "Thought I'd take the dog off your hands."

"What about the owner? Won't she be coming back?"

"If she does, let me know."

Doc Robinson took off his glasses and polished them slowly between the thumb and index finger of one hand. Then he put them on, went behind the desk and pulled out a file drawer. He wrote out a receipted bill, gave it to Novak and went through the paneled door that led to the kennels.

Novak laid a ten-dollar bill on the desk and folded the receipt into his pocket. He lighted a cigarette, and after a while the vet came back with the Skye terrier on a gray leather leash. Handing the leash to Novak he said, "What do you want a dog for, Pete?"

"Company. Good night, Doc."

Novak opened the door, and the little Skye bounded out to the wet sidewalk. When the leash checked it, it stopped and looked up at Novak. Novak reached down and stroked the dog's shaggy ears. Straightening, he turned back toward Seventeenth Street. The Skye yipped and scurried along beside him. Novak looked down and murmured, "Two forgotten men." Then he turned up Seventeenth Street toward the place where he lived.

Get Hard Case Crime by Mail...
And Save 43%!

☐ **YES! Sign me up for the Hard Case Crime Book Club!**

As long as I choose to stay in the club, I will receive every Hard Case Crime book as it is published (generally one each month). I'll get to preview each title for 10 days. If I decide to keep it, I will pay only $3.99* — a savings of 43% off the cover price! There is no minimum number of books I must buy and I may cancel my membership at any time.

Name: _____

Address: _____

City / State / ZIP: _____

Telephone: _____

E-Mail: _____

☐ **I want to pay by credit card:** ☐ VISA ☐ MasterCard ☐ Discover

Card #: _____ Exp. date: _____

Signature: _____

Mail this page (or a photocopy of it) to:

HARD CASE CRIME BOOK CLUB
20 Academy Street, Norwalk, CT 06850-4032

Or fax it to 610-995-9274.
You can also sign up online at www.dorchesterpub.com.

* Plus $2.00 for shipping. Offer open to residents of the U.S. and Canada only. Canadian residents please call 1-800-481-9191 for pricing information.

If you are under 18, a parent or guardian must sign. Terms, prices, and conditions subject to change. Subscription subject to acceptance. Dorchester Publishing reserves the right to reject any order or cancel any subscription.